AN EVANS NOVEL OF THE WEST

TARGETT

ROBERT J. RANDISI

M. Evans & Company, Inc.

Library of Congress Cataloging-in-Publication Data

Randisi, Robert J.
    Targett / Robert J. Randisi
        p.   cm.—(An Evans novel of the West)
    ISBN 0-87131-654-4 : $16.95
    I. Title.   II. Series.
  PS3568.A53T37   1991
  813'.54—dc20   91-13036
                                                                  CIP

M. Evans and Company, Inc.
216 East 49th Street
New York, New York 10017

Manufactured in the United States of America

9 8 7 6 5 4 3 2 1

Prologue
Silverton, California

Targett moved quietly down the alley, his gun in his hand. He'd found out that the senator's son was being held in a room upstairs from the Silverton Saloon. He had come from San Francisco to find the kidnapped twenty-one-year-old son of a United States senator. It was not the kind of job he usually took. In this case he had left it up to the senator to put a price on his son's life, and it had been too generous a price to pass up—even with the odd stipulation tagged onto the end of it.

He reached the rear of the Silverton and moved to the back door. He could hear the music and voices coming from inside, and it was all loud enough to cover the noise he made forcing the door.

Once inside he found himself in a hallway that ran from left to right. If he went left it would take him to the main part of the saloon. To the right he could see a flight of steps leading up, and he went that way, ascending the steps as quietly as he could.

In the upstairs hall he paused and listened. He could still hear the sounds of reverie from downstairs, and for a moment he enter-

1

tained the thought of going down and joining the crowd. They sounded like they were having a real good time.

Dispelling the thought with a shake of his head he started down the long hall, listening at doors as he went along. Behind more than one he heard the sounds of a man and woman partaking in an age-old form of recreation and he continued along until he reached a door where he heard no sounds at all. He turned the doorknob and found the door unlocked. He entered quickly with his gun held out in front of him, but the room was empty. He backed out and continued checking each door in sequence. He finally came to a locked door that had no sounds coming from behind it. Again, thanks to the noise from downstairs, no one was able to hear when he forced his entrance.

As he entered the room he saw a young man on the bed, tied and gagged. He closed the door behind him and holstered his gun. Then he moved to the bed and removed the man's gag.

"Are you Joe Baker?"

"Yes," the man said hoarsely.

"Senator Adam Bennett Baker's son?"

The man on the bed frowned. "My father's middle name is not Bennett," he said. "It's Gordon."

Senator Baker had said that only members of his family would know that.

Joseph Baker was tied hand and foot to the bed, so Targett untied him and helped him sit up.

"Are you injured?"

"No," Baker replied.

"Can you ride?"

"Yes."

"All right," Targett said, "we're going to walk out of here and over to the livery, where I have two horses waiting for us. If anyone gets in our way, I will take care of them. Is that understood?"

"Yes."

"Let's go, then."

Targett went to the door and opened it a crack so he could look down the hall. He then opened it further so he could stick his head out and look the other way. He stepped into the hall and waved to Baker to follow him. He left his gun in his holster because even if they were confronted by one or two men, a shot would alert all the others. He would try and handle a small number of men with his hands, as quickly and silently as possible.

They walked to the back of the hall without incident and were making their way down the steps just as two men appeared at the bottom. The two were about to set foot on the steps when they looked up.

"Hey," one of them said, frowning, "ain't that the kid?" he pointed at Targett and Baker.

The other one frowned, too, and said, "Ain't he supposed to be locked up?"

Targett continued down and said, "He sure is. Are you two supposed to be watching him?"

"Well . . . yeah . . ." one answered.

"We just went downstairs for a little drink," the other one said.

"And he got loose and got out," Targett stated. "How do you suppose that happened?"

"I don't—" one of them started to say, but by that time Targett had reached them. His feet were about level with their faces, so he kicked out. The squared toe of his boot caught one man flush on the chin. His head snapped back with an audible crack and he sank to the floor. The other man was so busy watching him fall that he didn't see Targett's left hand as it removed a heavy baton from a leather thong on his left hip. Targett swung the stick, cracking the man's head open and killing him instantly. He slid the stick back into the thong without taking the time to savor the satisfying vibration that had traveled up his arm when the stick had impacted with the man's head.

"Come on," Targett told Baker.

They stepped over the kidnappers and Targett led the way to the back door. As he opened it a man came into the hall from the other direction, but he was not as slow-witted as the first two men were.

He went for his gun immediately.

Fortunately for Targett the man's move was not particularly fast and Targett was able to free his gun of leather before the newcomer was. Targett fired once and the bullet knocked the man back against the wall.

"Come on!" Targett shouted, not waiting to watch the body fall.

He hoped that the noise in the saloon would either cause the men there to *miss* the shot, or at least keep them from reacting at once. The sound of a single shot could always be mistaken for something else, and Targett hoped that would happen this time.

Targett and Baker had run down the alley and were on the main street running toward the livery when Targett heard the men emptying out of the Silverton.

"There they go!" someone yelled.

"They're gonna kill us," Joseph Baker shouted.

"Only if you stop running," Targett said from behind him. "Now keep going to the livery."

They both kept running and when they reached the livery two saddled horses were waiting for them.

"What's the matter?" the liveryman asked, but Targett did not pause to answer. He grabbed the reins of his horse and mounted up.

"Hey," the liveryman shouted, "you ain't paid!"

Baker mounted the other horse and he and Targett rode out of town on a dead-run.

"What about them?" he asked Targett.

"Most of them will have to saddle up to chase us, and they're going to be disappointed."

"Why?"

"I cut through the cinches on all the saddles in the livery except these two."

Baker smiled for the first time since Targett had freed him, and then let out a war whoop.

"Keep riding," Targett said. "Some of them will have had horses in front of the saloon, already saddled."

If they had, however, they were not anxious to chase Baker and whoever had freed him and handled three men with only one shot fired—not without the help of the rest of the men, who were unable to saddle up.

They rode through the night and stopped to rest on high ground, from where Targett could see they were not being followed.

"I can't believe you just walked into the Silverton and cut me free," Baker said. "There were at least twenty men in there."

"They may have found themselves saddles by now, so you'll have to keep riding a spell."

"Me? Where are you going?"

"I'm heading that way," Targett said, pointing east.

"Well, I'll go with you."

"No," Targett said, "you won't."

"But you rescued me."

"Your father hired me to rescue you."

"And bring me back?"

"No," Targett replied. Now he was coming to the odd stipulations the senator had set.

Targett reached into his saddlebags and pulled out two items. "The senator wanted me to give you these, and send you on your way on your own," he said.

Baker put out his hand and accepted first a small sack that was obviously filled with coins, and then a handgun and holster.

"But—"

"He wanted me to tell you to pick your friends a little more wisely, and not to go bragging that you're the son of a senator, or before long he'll be getting another ransom note—and he won't pay."

"I don't understand."

"I was sent to the coordinates where I was supposed to drop the ransom. There was a man waiting there to collect, but I, uh, persuaded him to tell me where you were. My job was to get you out and send you off on your own, and that's what I'm doing."

"Look, mister . . ."

Targett did not supply his name.

"Mister, you could let me ride with you, couldn't you? I mean, my father wouldn't know."

"I'd know," Targett said. "When I hire on to do a job I do it, and no more. You're on your own, kid. Take my advice and take your *father's* advice."

"Hey—" Joseph Baker said, but he was cut off when Targett's fist smashed into his face, knocking him from his horse.

Targett dismounted at his leisure and caught the boy just as he was lifting himself up off the ground.

"H-hey—" Baker said again, weakly. Targett reached for him, straightened him up, and then hit him again. The younger man went over backward, hitting the ground hard. Targett looked down at him for a moment, convinced that he wasn't getting up. This was part of the job, too, a parting message from his father *not* to cause him trouble in the future.

Targett went over to the fallen man, leaned over, grabbed him by the hair and lifted his head from the ground.

"Take your father's advice," he said into Baker's ear, and then dropped his head to the ground. He turned to walk away, then turned back and kicked Baker in the ribs—hard!

One for the road, he thought.

Targett mounted up and rode off, not bothering to look back.

One

Targett rode into Dodge early in the morning, so there wasn't a lot of activity on Front Street. Even quiet, however, Dodge City was impressive. Just during his ride to the livery he saw four good-sized saloon and gambling houses—the Lady Gay, the Alamo, the Lone Star, and the largest, the Long Branch—three restaurants, and three hotels—the biggest being Dodge House. In addition there was every kind of store imaginable—general store, hardware store, haberdashery store, stores that sold guns, lumber, feed, shoes, and there was even a pharmacy and a theater. Besides all this he saw more two-story buildings than he had ever seen in a western town. Dodge City was almost as much a city as San Francisco was—on a smaller scale, of course.

He rode to the livery at the end of Front Street and turned his horse over to the liveryman, a man in his late twenties who had a ready, friendly smile.

"Stayin' a while?" the man asked.

"Just passing through," Targett said, "but I might stay a few days."

"Know anybody hereabouts?"

"I do if Bat Masterson is still sheriff here."

"Afraid you're out of luck," the man said. "Bat moved on some months ago."

"Oh? That's a shame. Who replaced him?"

"Sheriff Pat Sughrue, but Bill Tilghman is still under-sheriff, although there's some talk about him being offered the job of city marshal by Mayor Wright."

"Is that a fact?" Targett knew of Tilghman, but had never met him. "Well, since I'm here I suppose I'll have a look around, anyway."

"Town's not as wide open as it was before Bat Masterson took the job as sheriff and hired Tilghman as under-sheriff right away, but there's still lots to do hereabouts, lots to do."

"I can just imagine," Targett said.

The man put his hand down and said, "Name's Tom Nixon."

Targett took the hand, shook it, and said, "Targett."

"Just Targett?" Nixon asked, curiously.

Target nodded and repeated, "Just Targett."

While Targett was at the livery under-sheriff Bill Tilghman and Mayor Bob Wright were having an early breakfast in the dining room of the Dodge House.

"Things may not be as wild as when Bat was sheriff, Bill," Wright said, "but we still need more law enforcement than the sheriff's office can provide—especially when the drives come in."

"I understand that, Mr. Mayor," Tilghman said.

Wright was the owner of the largest general store in town, and Tilghman—not yet thirty—had not only built himself a reputation as a lawman, but had his own ranch in Bluff Creek, Kansas. He had hired a man to run his ranch when he had moved to Dodge with his wife, Flora, to take the job as Bat Masterson's under-sheriff.

"I've managed to convince the town council to allow a budget for city marshal, and a deputy."

Tilghman frowned. "How does Pat feel about all this?" he asked, referring to Sheriff Pat Sughrue.

"He's objecting violently, but only to the fact that he'd be losing you as under-sheriff. He realizes, however, that this is no reflection on him as a lawman."

"I see," Tilghman said.

"We'll have a proper badge made up for you and everything."

Tilghman nodded, pouring himself another cup of coffee, and then one for the mayor.

"Do you want some time to think it over, Bill?" Wright asked.

"This offer hasn't exactly been a secret, Mr. Mayor," Tilghman said.

"I know," Wright said, his mouth giving way to an embarrassed smile. "it's been in the air for quite some time."

"As it happens," Tilghman went on, "I have already thought about what I would do if and when the offer did come."

"And?"

Tilghman picked up his coffee cup and said, "And I decided that I would accept."

"Wonderful!" Wright said, enthusiastically.

"Under one condition."

Wright frowned and said, "That being?"

"I name my own deputy, with no interference from you or the council."

"As long as he's a competent man I see no problem with that."

"Then let's drink to it," Tilghman said, and raised his coffee cup to his lips.

Forgetting that Tilghman did not drink, Wright said, "Later on I'll buy you a proper drink to seal the deal, but this will have to do for now."

Targett decided to treat himself to the best and biggest hotel in Dodge, Dodge House. When he entered he was again struck by the similarity between this town and San Francisco. The lobby of the Dodge House, in its own way, was posh and impressive. He walked to the front desk and set his saddlebags and rifle on the floor.

"Good morning, sir," the clerk said. "Would you like a room?"

All desk clerks went to the same school, and Targett always felt like answering that question with: "No, I'll just bunk here in the lobby." Instead he said, "Yes, I'd like a room."

"Very good, sir," the clerk said. He turned the register around so Targett could sign in and asked, "How many nights will you be with us, sir?"

"I'm not sure," Targett said, signing the register: *Targett, San Francisco, California.*

"Well, sir, however long your stay with us is, we hope you enjoy it."

"If I don't," Targett said, accepting the key, "it will be my own fault."

Targett was about to turn and go up the stairs when he saw two men standing in the doorway to the dining room, both eyeing him.

"Excuse me," Targett said to the clerk, "who are those two gentlemen?"

The clerk looked and said, "The older man with the grey mustache is Mayor Wright, and the younger man with the bushy mustache is under-sheriff Bill Tilghman."

"Tilghman, huh?"

"Yes, sir."

Targett gave Tilghman one last steady look, then picked up his rifle and saddlebags and went up the stairs to the second floor.

Tilghman and Mayor Wright had spotted Targett registering at the front desk, just as they were leaving the dining room.

"A stranger," Tilghman said.

"*He* rode into town early," Wright noted.

"He's got the look."

"What look is that?" the mayor asked.

Without taking his eyes off the man at the desk Tilghman said, "Trouble."

"Why don't you go and talk to him?"

Tilghman looked at Wright and said, "As under-sheriff, or as city marshal?"

"Well, technically," Mayor Bob Wright said, "you won't be city marshal until we swear you in and give you your badge."

"Which will be when?"

"Tomorrow."

Tilghman gave the mayor a surprised look.

"We're already having the badge made up," Wright said. "I knew you'd take the job."

"Maybe you know me too well, Mayor," Tilghman said, looking at the big man at the desk.

Tilghman held the man's gaze while the stranger spoke to the clerk again, obviously asking who the two men staring at him were. Once the stranger knew whom he was dealing with he turned and went upstairs.

"I have to get back to my office," Wright said when the new-comer was gone.

"I'll just take a look at the register before I leave," Tilghman said, "and I'll let the sheriff know there's a stranger in town."

Wright walked out the front door while Tilghman went to the desk and read the register. He did not recognize the name, but thought it odd that the man had only signed one name, with no indication whether it was his first or last.

He asked the clerk about him.

"Didn't talk much," the clerk said, "but he was interested in who you were."

"Well, that makes us even," Tilghman said, "because I am interested in who he is."

Two

Bill Tilghman left the hotel and went directly to the sheriff's office. Pat Sughrue was sitting behind his desk and scowled at Tilghman as the younger man entered.

Sughrue had been under a lot of pressure after taking over as sheriff from Bat Masterson, but despite Sughrue's only being in office a short time he had proven to be up to the job. Of course, had Dodge City been the place it was before Masterson, many thought Sughrue would not have done as well as he had so far.

"Well, if it isn't the new city marshal of Dodge City," Sughrue said.

"How do you know I took the job?"

"You have one glaring fault, my lad," Sughrue said to Tilghman.

"And what is that?"

"Your inability to say no."

Tilghman would like to have argued, but he had been told the very same thing too many times by his wife, and so had little ammunition for argument.

"I like being needed," he said lamely.

"*I* need you," Sughrue said.

"The good of the town comes before the good of the individual, Pat."

"What kind of bonehead will I get this time for under-sheriff?"

"A bonehead of your own choosing."

"Which brings me to the question of who *your* deputy will be?" Sughrue asked, curiously.

"I have a man in mind," Tilghman admitted, "but I would rather not comment until I have asked him."

"Fair enough," Sughrue said. "When will you be appointed?"

"Tomorrow."

"Are you too good to make some rounds on your last day as under-sheriff?"

"No, Pat," Tilghman said, "if there is anything I am not it is *too* good."

"Then get out of here."

"One more thing."

"What? You want to turn this into the marshal's office?"

Sughrue's joke made Tilghman realize that he had not asked about an office. He assumed he would have one, but where?

"A stranger was registering at the hotel when I left there."

"Did you get a name?"

"Targett, from San Francisco."

"Just Targett?"

Tilghman shrugged and said, "That's all he signed."

"Now what's he hiding?" Sughrue wondered aloud.

"Maybe just a first name he doesn't like, but I thought I'd send a telegram to San Francisco."

"Why? Why not just ask him?"

"I don't know," Tilghman said. "I have a different feeling about this one."

"All right, then," Sughrue said, "you handle it . . . Marshal."

"Pat, about this marshal thing—"

Sughrue held his hand up to ward off unnecessary explanations.

"I understand the town's position, Bill. There's no need for you or I to fuss over this."

"I appreciate that, Pat," Bill said. "I'll go and make rounds."

"You do that," Sughrue said. "I think I'll take advantage of my superior position—temporary though it may be—to put my feet up and catch a nap."

"Sleep well," Tilghman said, and left.

Targett left his belongings in the room and then went downstairs to have a bath and a meal—in that order.

After the bath he changed into clean clothes and asked the desk clerk if he could get his old clothes cleaned.

"Yes, sir," the clerk said, "just leave them with me and we'll have them cleaned and returned to you in your room."

"Thank you."

Targett entered the dining room, and had a lavish breakfast of steak and eggs, which was prepared to perfection.

As he ate he thought about Bill Tilghman. Targett had heard of the young man from Masterson and Luke Short, both of whom were greatly impressed with Tilghman as a buffalo hunter and lawman. Targett himself was impressed with the way Tilghman had held his gaze in the lobby. Targett was not a modest man. He knew he presented a fearsome countenance at times, especially after days on the trail. He was a big, fair-haired, dangerous-looking man, and Tilghman had not backed down a bit from his stare. Also, Tilghman had instantly recognized him for what he was—a man who made his living from danger. That kind of man can bring trouble with him to any town he passes through, and Tilghman knew that.

Targett would have been surprised if Tilghman had not gotten his name from the register and was at that very moment sending a telegram to San Francisco.

Targett decided that he would just sit back, enjoy Dodge City, and wait for Tilghman to come to him.

Tilghman sent his telegram and told the clerk to find him when the answer came in. Then he left the telegraph office and went to the livery stable.

"Hello, Bill," Tom Nixon said.

"Tom."

Since Bat Masterson's departure from Dodge City, Tom Nixon had become Tilghman's closest friend. He was also a man Tilghman would trust with his back.

"Stranger rode in today," Tilghman said. "Know anything about him?"

"His name's Targett," Nixon said. "He came looking for Bat."

"For Bat? Why?"

"I assumed they were friends," Nixon said.

"Did he say that?"

Nixon thought a moment, then replied, "No. I asked if he knew anyone in Dodge and he said that he did if Bat was still sheriff."

"Nothing was said about being friends."

"No . . . why?"

"I'm just curious about him, is all," Tilghman said. "He signed in the register at the Dodge House as 'Targett.' No first or last name."

"I asked him about that," Nixon said. "Asked him if it was just Targett and that's what he said, 'Just Targett.'"

"Maybe his first name's Just," Tilghman said, and Nixon laughed.

"You come over here 'just' to talk about Targett?" Nixon asked.

"No, I came over to tell you that I've accepted the position as city marshal."

"Well, I'm sure *that's* a surprise to everyone concerned," Nixon said teasingly.

"I did make one condition."

"What was that?"

"That I be allowed to name my own deputy."

"I don't see where that would be a problem. I'm sure they know you'd pick a competent man."

"You won't think so when I tell you who I'm going to name."

"Oh?" Nixon said, curious. "Why? Who are you going to name?"

"You'd better get somebody to run this dump for a while," Tilghman said, looking around. "By ten o'clock tomorrow morning I'll be city marshal and," he added, looking at his friend now, "by 10:01 I will have sworn *you* in as my deputy."

Three

In keeping with his decision to stay at the best hotel in Dodge Targett decided that his drinking and gambling would be done at the largest bar, the Long Branch. When he entered he saw the longest bar he had ever seen. It was noon, so there was plenty of space at the bar. He walked to the end nearest him and watched the burly bartender head toward him.

"What'll it be?"

"Beer."

"Comin' up."

The bartender drew the beer and placed it in front of Targett. He took a deep swallow and found it ice-cold. With beer in hand he studied the interior of the Long Branch.

It was a very big place, with crystal chandeliers and plenty of tables. Along one wall were the blackjack and faro tables, and on the back wall was a roulette wheel. There were enough tables that several of them were probably used for house-dealt poker games when evening came. Poker was Targett's game when he gambled, which he felt no compulsion to do. It was something he did to relax and enjoy.

"When do the tables open?" he asked the bartender.

"General about four o'clock, unless we get a call for it, then we put someone on them earlier."

"Dealers any good?"

"We got one of the best," the bartender said. "Ben Thompson."

Targett had heard of Thompson. He'd been in Abilene when Hickok was marshal there. He'd gone on to make a name for himself for being both a good man with a gun and with a deck of cards.

"You just get into town?" the barman asked.

"That's right."

"Stayin'?"

"A day or two."

"Good gambling here," the man went on, "and fine women."

Targett wasn't sure if the man was using "here" to describe Dodge City, or the Long Branch in particular.

"That's what I hear."

"'Course, you should have seen this town in the old days, before Masterson cleaned it up."

"Wide open, eh?"

"You said it, mister," the bartender said, and the gleam in his eyes said that he missed those days dearly. "This used to be one hell of a town for gamblers let me tell you—and we still got some of the best. Thompson, Dick Clark. Luke Short used to own the Red Dog Saloon before he left."

Targett remembered about Short now that the bartender had mentioned it. He had seen the man in San Francisco last year, and had forgotten that the man owned a saloon in Dodge.

"This used to be some town," the bartender repeated, shaking his head.

"I'm sorry I never got a chance to see it," Targett said, and he meant it.

"Where you from?"

"San Francisco."

"Say," the bartender said with a smile, "I hear that's a great town for gamblers."

"Big-money gamblers," Targett said.

"You ever see Masterson there?"

"Sure," Targett said, "Luke Short, too."

Knowing that Targett had gambled with those men seemed to move him up in the bartender's estimation.

"Hey, how about another, on the house?"

"Sure," Targett said, pushing the empty mug towards the man. "Pour away."

While Targett was having his second beer at the Long Branch, Bill Tilghman was reading the reply to his telegraph message.

"What's the story?" Pat Sughrue asked.

"It seems our friend Mr. Targett has quite a reputation in San Francisco as a man who can get things done."

"What kind of things?" Sughrue asked, frowning.

Tilghman looked up from the telegram and said, "Anything. According to this, he's not a lawbreaker, but he's bent it from time to time."

"Who is the telegram from?"

"San Francisco police," Tilghman said, handing it over. "According to them he doesn't look for trouble, but it generally finds him, whether he's working or not."

"It doesn't say exactly what he does for a living," Sughrue pointed out.

"Maybe I'll have to get that from Mr. Targett myself," Tilghman said. "That, and whether he's here on business or pleasure."

"Why not have Nixon brace him tomorrow," Sughrue suggested. "You know, baptism by fire?"

"I don't need to test Tom Nixon, Pat," Tilghman said. "Besides, I want to meet Mr. Targett myself."

Four

Targett was sitting alone at a table in the crowded Long Branch later that evening when Bill Tilghman walked in. He heard people congratulating the man on being named city marshal. Tilghman appeared to be very popular in Dodge City.

Targett was nursing a beer, watching the saloon fill up. He watched the gaming tables open, he watched the women come out and start working the floor. The dealers were smooth, but the women were even smoother. The Long Branch seemed to hire only stunning women; some because of their faces, some because of their figures, but they all had something that would appeal to men, and Targett was enjoying watching them work.

Tilghman went to the bar and got himself a beer—Targett noticed that he paid for it—and had a short conversation with the bartender. The under-sheriff-turned-city marshal turned his back to the bar and regarded the room, acknowledging greetings from people. Slowly, Tilghman surveyed the room and then his eyes finally came to rest on Targett.

As Targett had suspected, Tilghman finally pushed away from the bar and started across the room toward him.

"Hello, Marshal," Targett said as Tilghman reached him.

"I won't be marshal until tomorrow," Tilghman said.

"I'm giving you the benefit of the doubt."

"Mind if I sit down and get acquainted?"

Targett shrugged.

"It's your town."

Tilghman pulled back a chair and sat down, putting his beer down on the bar. Targett noticed that the lawman had not yet taken a drink from the mug.

"I understand you're friends with Bat Masterson," Tilghman said.

"Who told you that?"

"Why? Aren't you friends with him?"

"No."

"But you came here looking for him."

Targett leaned forward slightly and said, "Now who told you that?"

Tilghman didn't answer, and he didn't take a sip from his drink.

"Why don't we stop playing games?" Tilghman finally said. "You told the liveryman that you were here looking for Bat Masterson."

"No I didn't."

"I thought we were going to stop play—"

"*He* asked *me* if I knew anyone in town and I said I did, *if* Bat Masterson was still the sheriff—which, I understand, he is not."

"So you *know* Bat Masterson, but you're not friends," Tilghman said.

"That's the first correct thing you've said since you came over here."

"Well, if you're not friends with Bat, what are you—enemies?"

"No," Targett said. "We've played cards together from time to time, we've backed each other's play from time to time. That makes us . . . acquaintances."

"And what about Luke Short?"

"Same deal," Targett said. "Actually, I almost like Short."

"And Masterson?"

"I can't say that for Masterson."

"Bat's a good friend of mine."

Targett shrugged.

"He's a little too slick for me."

Tilghman smiled. "That's Bat's style, and I know everyone doesn't like it."

"That's very understanding of you."

"Now I have a new question for you."

"Go ahead."

"What are you doing in Dodge?"

"I was on a job near here and decided to come and see what it was like. I've heard so much about it."

"What you heard was from the old days."

"Yeah, I heard about the old days from the bartender." Targett said. "He told you about me and Short, huh?"

"Yes."

"And the liveryman told you about Masterson."

"Right."

"And what did you find out from your telegram to San Francisco?"

"How did you know about that?"

"It's what I would have done."

Tilghman nodded, accepting that.

"All I found out from the San Francisco police is that you're a law *bender*, but not a law *breaker*."

"Nice of them to make the distinction."

"I hope you're not planning to *bend* any laws while you're here."

"The thought hadn't occurred to me."

"Good," Tilghman said. "How long do you plan to stay in town?"

"I don't know," Targett said. "I guess as long as the town amuses me."

"Well, there are a lot of ways to be amused in Dodge City—legally," Tilghman said, standing up. "I hope that's all you were thinking of."

Targett looked at the man's beer, which was untouched.

"Aren't you going to drink that?"

"Not me," Tilghman said. "I don't drink. I brought that over for you." With a smile he said, "Enjoy."

Five

The next morning Bill Tilghman was sworn in as marshal of Dodge City. Mayor Wright handed him his badge. A twenty-dollar gold piece had been hung from a gold bar. On the front it read: *CITY MARSHAL*. On the back was written the current year and: *WILLIAM TILGHMAN, FROM YOUR MANY FRIENDS, DODGE CITY.*

Tilghman in turn swore Tom Nixon in as his deputy, and issued only one order: "Tom, we've got to give Dodge a new reputation. I want it to be known as a town you can't shoot up."

That statement impressed the town council, and Tom Nixon, who agreed.

"Where is my office to be?" Tilghman asked.

"In this building," Wright said. They were in the town hall. "We've emptied out a room on the second floor and put in a desk. Uh, I'm afraid it's a very old desk."

"That's all right," Tilghman said.

"You'll have to share jail cells with the sheriff," Wright said, his tone still apologetic.

"I'm sure the sheriff won't mind," Tilghman said. "I'd like to go to work now."

"Good," Wright said. He shook hands with Tilghman and said, "Good luck."

The rest of the town council filed out, shaking hands with the new marshal and his deputy.

"Well," Tilghman said, after the others had gone, "let's go see that office."

"I hope it has a coffee pot," Nixon said.

"At least," Tilghman said.

They went up to the second floor and looked for the office.

"Is that it?" Tilghman asked, pointing to a door.

Nixon opened it, shook his head and said, "Broom closet," closing the door.

They continued down the upstairs hallway until they found a door marked *CITY MARSHAL*.

"They could have put your name on it," Nixon said.

"That would make extra work when they fire me," Tilghman said.

"Fire you?" Nixon queried.

Tilghman pointed to the words on the door and said, "This just indicates how fleeting the trust of the people can be."

Tilghman opened the door and they entered. The room was not large, but at least it was bigger than the broom closet.

The desk was against a wall. The top of it was pitted, scarred, and dusty.

"They could have cleaned the room," Tom Nixon said, running his finger through the dust on the desktop.

"We'll have to get someone to take care of that," Tilghman said.

He walked around the desk and sat in the straight-backed wooden chair that had been placed behind it. Sheriff Sughrue had a swivel chair on wheels.

"Where am I supposed to sit?" Nixon asked.

"It doesn't matter," Tilghman said. "We'll rarely be here at the same time. We'll cover the town in two twelve-hour shifts. I'll take three in the afternoon until three in the morning."

"I gotta get up at two A.M.?" Nixon exclaimed, but realized that the shift Tilghman was taking for himself was the one where there was the most potential for trouble.

"We all have our crosses to bear, Tom," Tilghman said, spreading his hands. "I'll be up during prime drinking hours—and I don't drink."

"Maybe you should start," Nixon suggested.

Tilghman looked around the room, which was bare but for the desk and chair. The only window in the room looked out over the garbage behind the building.

"Maybe I should," he mussed, "maybe I should."

While Bill Tilghman was being sworn in, Targett was having breakfast. He had risen late to find a warm hip pressed against his. It took him a moment to identify the hip's owner, one of the "stunning" girls from the Long Branch, who looked less stunning in the morning. She was one of the ones whose body was her best feature, and the morning did not do wonders for her rather plain face. She showed him, however—once he woke her up—that although her face was plain her mouth was quite educated.

He left her in the room when he went down for breakfast because she told him with a smile, "I've already had my breakfast, dear."

He decided there was nothing in the room for her to steal, so there was no harm in leaving her there. He left some money on the dresser for her and went out.

As he walked down the steps to the lobby he realized he couldn't remember her name, and thought it was best that he not go back and ask her.

Over breakfast he wondered if he should bother staying in Dodge at all. He still was not anxious to get back to San Francisco, but maybe he should just wander about some in the general direction of San Francisco, and take his time getting there.

He was facing the doorway of the dining room and saw the girl when she left. She still was a bit disheveled, but looked better than she had when she first woke up.

He decided to stay long enough to try one more girl from the

Long Branch. Targett was not a ladies man, so most of the women he dallied with were no ladies.

After breakfast he walked down to the livery to check on his horse. If he was going to leave in the morning—*if*, indeed, he was going to leave then—he wanted to make sure his horse would be ready to travel.

When he entered he noticed an older man instead of the one he'd met the day before, Tom Nixon.

"What happened to the other guy?" he asked.

"Tom Nixon? He's got hisself a new job."

"Is that a fact?"

"Sure is," the old man said. "Bill Tilghman named him his deputy marshal. You heard about Bill being named city marshal?"

"I heard," Targett said. "I'd like to check on my horse."

"Leaving?"

"Maybe tomorrow morning."

"Which is he?"

"The dappled grey."

"Oh, that one."

"Why?" Targett asked, frowning.

"Found some filling in his left front this morning."

"Can I see?"

The man walked Targett back to his horse's stall and Targett ran his hand over the horse's leg. Sure enough there was some swelling just above the ankle, and he could feel heat, as well.

"I guess I won't be leaving in the morning," Targett said, turning to the man. "You know how to treat that?"

"Sure do," the man said. "I'll have to pack it—"

"Then do it," Targett said, cutting him before he could go through the entire procedure. "I'll check back on him in a couple of days."

"You want to trade him for another horse?"

"You got one around that's as good as he is?"

The old man rubbed his jaw and said, "Not for trade. You might

30

have to sell yours and then buy another. There's a couple of dealers in town—"

"Never mind," Targett said, "I'll wait until he heals proper."

"Sure thing. Other than the ankle he's a fine-looking animal."

"I know."

Targett did not own a horse. Whenever he had to leave San Francisco he usually did so by train, and then bought a horse along the way. Then, somewhere enroute back to San Francisco, he'd sell it. He never rented one because he never knew if he was going to get back to the point where he rented it.

He had been so satisfied with this animal's performance, though, that he was actually considering taking the horse back to San Francisco with him.

"I guess leaving tomorrow just wasn't in the cards," he said aloud.

"You a gambler?" the old man asked. "Lots of games in town."

"I know," Targett said, "and I guess I'll have to play some of them to pass the time."

Six

When Targett was walking back from the livery he saw Bill Tilghman and Tom Nixon leaving town hall. He was on the same side of the street, so there was no way to avoid them without overtly crossing the street—and there was really no reason to do that.

When both men turned and saw Targett coming toward them he could see the gold badge on Tilghman's chest.

"Nice badge," Targett said.

"Have you decided to stay in town a while?" Tilghman asked.

"Had the decision made for me," Targett said. He looked at Nixon and said, "My horse has developed a filling in his left front leg, just above the ankle."

"Swollen?" Nixon said.

"And there's some heat," Targett said. "That fella you've got there, does he know what he's doing?"

"Taught me everything I know about horses," Nixon said. "He'll take care of your animal better than anyone else in town could."

"I'll take your word for that."

Nixon noticed the way Targett and Tilghman were sizing each other up and decided to try and melt the tension between them. They were like two roosters eyeing each other in the farm yard.

"We were just gonna get some coffee over at your hotel," Nixon said to Targett. "Join us?"

Targett looked from Tilghman to Nixon and said, "Sure, why not? Can't hurt to get in good with the law if I'm gonna stay in town a while, right?"

Nixon knew that Tilghman would not accept that statement in the spirit in which it was given, so he stepped in before Tilghman could reply and said, "Since you're buying it's us who will be getting in good with you."

Targett eyed Nixon and said, "You've gotten the hand of this lawman stuff already, huh?"

They went over to the Dodge House and got a table in the dining room.

Nixon did most of the talking and after a half hour came to the decision that Targett and Tilghman would never be friends. They were just not operating on the same level. Tilghman was a stickler for the law, did not drink, and was married—*very* married.

Targett operated outside the law without breaking it. To Tilghman, *bending* and *breaking* were the same thing. Targett was cold and calculating, but Nixon detected a sense of humor beneath the cold surface—one that Bill Tilghman would never understand. And, of course, Targett drank, and had already told them of the woman who had awakened in his bed that morning.

"That would be Lisa," Nixon said. "Nice girl, firm body, but she's not the prettiest gal in town."

As the conversation turned in that direction Tilghman stood up and said, "I'm going to see about getting someone to clean that office, Tom. Mr. Targett, I assume I'll be seeing you around town."

"You assume correctly, Marshal."

Tilghman nodded and left.

"Jesus," Nixon said, "sitting at a table with the two of you is like sitting with a lit fuse."

"What do you mean?"

"You know what I mean," Nixon said. "You two mix together about as well as water and whiskey."

Targett didn't bother telling Nixon that a lot of men in San Francisco mixed water with their whiskey.

"Is he always like that?" Targett asked.

"Tilghman's a different breed than us, Targett," Nixon said. "He follows the law to the letter, feels it's important to enforce it that way. That man will die with a badge on his chest, but he'll probably be seventy years old when it happens."

"Lawmen don't live that long," Targett said.

"And do men in your business?"

"No."

"Well, Tilghman might be the exception."

"He really doesn't drink?"

"Doesn't drink, loves his wife, doesn't whore around, and he has a sense of humor, but you have to be his friend to see it."

"How many friends does he have?"

Nixon paused, then said, "That's a hard question to answer. He's *respected* by a lot of people, but I don't believe that he would refer to many of them as friends of his."

"You're his friend."

"That I am, and Bat Masterson is his friend. Beyond that . . ." Nixon said, and shrugged.

"How is he with a gun?"

"He's good, real good, but he's got something better than his ability with a gun."

"What's that?"

"He knows when to use it, and when not to."

Targett poured himself some more coffee, then offered more to Nixon, who nodded.

"You think a lot of him, don't you?" he asked.

"I think he's the finest man I know," Nixon said. "Mind you, he's not the most fun . . ."

"I wouldn't think so," Targett said. "So tell me about the girls at the Long Branch."

"Well, you've seen Tanya—"

"What one is she?"

"She's the brunette with the real pretty face, and the big—"

"Oh yeah, I've seen her . . ."

Bill Tilghman went to his house and told his wife, Flora, about the filthy office they had given him as city marshal.

"What did you expect?" she asked, looking at him wryly.

"Not much more," he said. "I'll have to find someone to clean it, though."

Now she crossed her arms and frowned at him mightily.

"On a regular basis, or just this once?"

"Well, of course we'll need someone on a regular basis, but I *would* like to have it cleaned real well the first time . . . by someone I trust."

"Bill Tilghman, you have no shame!" she said, shaking her head at the man she loved.

"Flora, I haven't asked—"

"Why don't you go and shine that nice new badge you got this morning," she said. "Don't come back to your office for a few hours. I'll have it scrubbed so clean the shine will blind you—but just this once!"

"Of course, dear," he said, taking her into his arms, "just this once."

Seven

The incident that led to Dodge City's new law started in the Long Branch that night. Targett had a peripheral part in it.

Targett had spent the day familiarizing himself with Dodge City. He walked around the entire town so that by dinner he could have given proper directions to almost anywhere in town.

He had dinner alone in the hotel dining room and then went to the Long Branch for an evening's entertainment.

He started by getting himself a beer and taking it to a back table. Lisa came by to say hello when she started work, obviously wanting to know if she would be leaving with Targett again that night, after the Long Branch closed. Targett pretended that he didn't know what she was up to and made small talk until she returned to work.

Targett did not want to make any commitment to Lisa until he talked to some of the other girls—specifically Tanya, the busty, pretty brunette that Tom Nixon had mentioned.

Targett and Nixon had talked for about another hour after Tilghman had left them that morning, and Targett found himself liking Nixon. Targett didn't like a lot of people, so it surprised him that he liked Nixon on such short acquaintance.

Nixon had told him that his shift would be over at three P.M., and he was going to have to get some sleep so he could relieve Tilghman at three A.M. He told Targett he would see him at the Long Branch, if Targett was still around that late.

Targett knew, therefore, that Tilghman would be in and out of the Long Branch all night, and he hoped that the new city marshal would not be giving him any special attention. Targett thought that he could dislike Tilghman as easily as he liked Nixon.

Targett watched as the saloon filled up. Many of the same people he had seen the night before were back again, doing the same things. A group of cowboys from a nearby ranch took a table for themselves and proceeded to drink whiskey down bottle after bottle. The same gamblers lined up at the faro and blackjack tables, and at the house poker games; open poker games appeared at some of the other tables. Lisa and Tanya and the other girls made their rounds, trying to pay an equal amount of attention to all of the customers so that no one would feel slighted. More than one saloon fight had started because of the attentions of a woman.

At one point Tanya came over and positioned herself in front of Targett's table, between him and the action in the room.

"You're a quiet one," she said, smiling at him. She was a big girl, about five-foot-ten, big-breasted, and wide-hipped. He knew that her thighs would be meaty and well-muscled. He wondered if Lisa had talked to her about him. He thought briefly of Lee, a waitress back in San Francisco with whom he might soon have a romance. Lee was the only woman he had ever thought of in those terms. These other women—Lisa, Tanya, saloon girls, and whores like them—he thought of only in terms of a night's distraction.

This one, Tanya, would surely make for a *full* night's distraction.

"Am I?" he finally spoke to her.

"Quieter than most. Mind if I sit down?"

"Go ahead."

Tanya pulled the chair opposite him out and sat down.

"You were here last night, too," she said. "I noticed you."

"I noticed you, too."

"Did you? You could have fooled me. I tried to catch your eyes several times but never succeeded."

"I must have been busy."

"Yes," Tanya said, "with Lisa."

"Well," Targett said, "she *was* in my lap."

Tanya laughed and said, "She *is* a little more forward than I am."

Targett looked past Tanya for a moment, because he didn't quite know what to say. He was usually comfortable with whores, because he knew what they wanted and they knew what he wanted. This one was different, and he felt some of his assurance slipping away.

"What will you be doing tonight, after closing?" she asked, finally.

He looked at her and said, "I don't know, for sure."

She smiled and stood up, then leaned over so that her generous breasts almost spilled out of her low-cut dress.

"Yes you do," she said, "for sure."

He watched her walk away to another table of men, but she only paused for a moment and then went on to the next one. He watched her stop at four or five more tables, but she never sat with anyone else.

He seemed to have been chosen, and he didn't mind at all.

With his activities after closing decided, Targett began to study all the games that were going on, and he decided to try Ben Thompson's blackjack table. He finished his beer and walked over. There was one empty chair at the table, and he took it.

Thompson, a good-looking man with a full mustache, looked up from his cards directly at Targett.

"Finally decided to get off your duff, eh?"

Targett took the comment as it was meant.

"I was getting sores."

"You saw last night what happens when you sit too long,"

Thompson said, "when Lisa flopped herself down in your lap. Guess you don't want that to happen again, huh?" The other men at the table laughed.

"I wouldn't mind if Lisa sat in my lap," one of them said.

"You gonna deal me some cards?" Targett asked Thompson.

"Oh, sure," the dealer said, "but I warn you, I don't roll over as easily as Lisa."

"We'll see."

They played for about an hour, and a run of luck—three hands of blackjack in a row—enabled Targett to come out even.

"That's it," Targett said, climbing off his stool.

"You quittin' hot?" Thompson asked. "Maybe there's a fourth blackjack hand in here."

"If there is," Targett said, "you give it to someone else. I'm not quitting, I'm just changing my game to something I know a lot better."

"What's that?" Thompson asked.

"Poker."

"Well," Thompson said, "stay out of the house game. Your odds are a lot better in one of the other games."

Targett knew that but said, "Thanks."

"Don't mention it."

Targett turned around and saw Tilghman standing at the bar, watching him. He waited until the new marshal inclined his head in acknowledgment and then nodded back.

He went over to the poker tables and saw that the two house games were very much under the house dealer's control. He decided not to try and buck them.

He went over to the other games and found two tables with an empty seat. He watched each game for about ten minutes, then chose one and took a seat. Nobody looked at him and no names were exchanged. All these men cared about was that there was another hand in the game. To most of them that meant that the cards might change, hopefully for the better.

The game was a dollar ante, with a two-dollar limit. Targett played poker for an hour and was a hundred dollars ahead. Those who were losing when he sat down had continued to lose. There was one other player who was winning, but not as much, since Targett entered the game.

"I don't like the way the cards changed when this fella sat down," one man said sourly.

"Take it easy, Mace," another man said. Targett had gotten the impression that both men worked together, on the same ranch.

The man named Mace was doing something Targett never did when he was gambling: he was drinking. He'd been a little drunk and morose when Targett sat down, and now he was *very* drunk and downright bitter about losing. Targett decided to take that into consideration and ignored the man's remarks.

"Him sittin' down should have changed the cards," Mace insisted. "My luck should have changed."

"It did," the other man who was winning said with a laugh, "it got worse."

"I don't need you to tell me my luck is bad!"

"Take it easy, Mace," his friend said, touching his arm.

"Don't touch my gun arm!" Mace said, yanking his arm away.

The man across the table mistook the move and thought that Mace was going for his gun. He kicked his chair back, drew his gun, and fired before Targett knew what had happened. His shot hit Mace in the shoulder, spinning him around and away from the table.

"Hey—" Mace's friend shouted, and the other man shot him, too. The bullet hit him square in the face and blew out the back of his head. The blood and brains splattered the table behind him, and the men who were sitting at it; the bullet kept going and hit one of *those* men in the shoulder.

"Take it easy!" Targett shouted, but he made no move toward the man. He knew by the look on the man's face that he'd shoot anything that moved.

Mace was sitting on the floor, bleeding from the right shoulder. He drew his gun with his wounded arm but he was so weak that his hand wavered when he squeezed the trigger. His shot went wild and hit one of the saloon girls in the arm.

"Jesus," Targett said. He looked around the room but Tilghman was no longer there. If he didn't do something a lot more people would get hurt.

Mace's dead friend was slumped in his chair. Targett used his right foot to tip the chair over, and the dead man fell on top of Mace. At the same time Targett used both hands to overturn the poker table towards the man who had started all the shooting. While he did that he came to his feet and drew his gun. The other man had been backing away from the table and now he tried to bring his gun around to bear on Targett. Targett swung his long arm in an arc and the barrel of his gun hit the man on the jaw, tearing it open. The man staggered back and dropped his gun.

At that moment Bill Tilghman came running in and the only man he saw holding a gun was Targett.

"Hold it right there, Targett!" he shouted, pointing his gun at Targett.

"Take it easy, Marshal," Targett said, reversing the gun in his hand an holding it up high, "it's all over."

Eight

"Four people shot," Tilghman said in disgust. "One dead—" he looked at Sheriff Pat Sughrue, who had just entered the room, and asked, "How is the girl?"

"She's all right. The doctor patched her up."

They were in Sughrue's office, since Tilghman obviously had no room in his, and also needed the jail cells.

"And the others?"

"Mace Cantwell's gonna be laid up for a while. Paul Rice, the man who was sitting at the other table, isn't hurt too bad."

"And the dead man's name?"

"Ross Spencer," Sughrue said. "He works with Cantwell at Hal Barton's ranch."

"And the man in the cell is Carl Martin."

"He started the shooting," Targett said.

It was the first thing he had said since entering the office. He had surrendered his gun to Tilghman at the saloon, when Tilghman had informed him that he was under arrest.

At that point several people, including Ben Thompson, had come forward to tell Tilghman that Targett had not fired a shot.

"Let's take this over to the sheriff's office and sort it out," Tilghman had said.

Now Tilghman, Sughrue, Targett, and Ben Thompson—as a representative of the Long Branch—were all in the office. Though the incident had taken place at two A.M., Tom Nixon was also present. He had come running when he heard the shooting. Carl Martin was already in a cell, and Tilghman had been ready to throw Targett into one, as well. Targett felt that Tilghman was disappointed that he had not been able to do so.

Ben Thompson had spoken first, testifying that Targett had not fired a shot, that he had prevented even more people from being injured.

"Fact is, Bill," Thompson said, "he did your job for you."

Tilghman didn't like that remark.

"And where were you when all this shooting was going on?" Tilghman demanded of Thompson.

"I was at my table," Thompson said, "across the room. There was a crowd of people between me and the action, so even if I had known what was happening, I couldn't have done anything."

"All right, Ben," Tilghman said. "You can go."

"You aren't going to arrest Targett?" Thompson asked.

"He tore Martin's face open," Tilghman said, "but no, I'm not going to arrest him. You can go."

Thompson stood up; without looking at Targett left the office.

Targett stood up and Tilghman said, "Where are you going?"

"If you're not arresting me—"

"Maybe I'm not putting you in a cell, but I'm not through with you yet."

Targett looked at Nixon, shrugged, and sat back down. After all, Tilghman had confiscated his gun and put it in a desk drawer.

"I asked you not to get into any trouble," Tilghman said, "and there you were tonight, right in the middle of it."

"I was playing poker," Targett said, "and doing very nicely, thank you."

"Did you have to tear Martin over like that?"

"He was going to shoot me next," Targett said. "I couldn't have that."

"Couldn't you have done something sooner?" Tilghman demanded. "Before so many people got hurt?"

Targett smiled tightly.

"Tilghman, either you wanted me to stay out of it, or you wanted me to do something sooner. You can't have it both ways."

"Look—" Tilghman started, but he held himself back.

Off to one side Sughrue and Nixon were exchanging glances. They knew that Targett was right, and that Tilghman was frustrated.

Finally, Tilghman opened a drawer of Sughrue's desk and took out Targett's gun and gunbelt.

"Here," he said, putting it on top of the desk, "take it and get out."

Targett stood up, took his time strapping on his gunbelt, and then started for the door. When he got there he turned around and looked at Tilghman.

"Don't bother to thank me," he said, and left.

Tilghman stood up and vacated Sughrue's chair, and the sheriff moved around and sat down.

"Bill, I know you don't like Targett—"

"I don't have anything against Targett personally," Tilghman said, "I just don't like his type."

"You've got to admit that Targett kept anyone else from being hurt," Tom Nixon said.

"If he was going to act, why didn't he act sooner?" Tilghman said. "Did he have to wait until a man was dead, and a woman was hurt? Or did he only act when *he* was personally threatened?"

"The point is, he didn't have to act at all," Sughrue said. "You jumped on him for doing so, and then you jumped on him for doing so too late."

"You can't have it both ways, Bill," Nixon said.

Tilghman glared at both men and said, "You're both taking his side, eh?"

"Bill—" Sughrue said.

Tilghman ignored the sheriff. He turned to Nixon and said, "You're on duty, Deputy. I'm going home."

As Tilghman went out the door Nixon shrugged helplessly at Sughrue.

"Maybe," Sughrue said, "it would be better for all concerned if Targett left Dodge City. BIll can't seem to think straight about him."

"I'll talk to Targett," Nixon said, "but his horse is lame."

"Maybe he'll take another one."

"I'll talk to him," Nixon repeated.

Nine

When Targett left the sheriff's office he started back to his hotel.

"Hey!"

He turned and saw the girl from the Long Branch, Tanya, running across the street toward him.

"Hello," he said when she reached him.

"You forgot something," she said.

He frowned and asked, "What?"

She had thrown a shawl over her bare shoulders, and now she opened it to reveal her cleavage and replied, "Me."

Targett had intended to go back to his room alone, but looking down at her cleavage—and *down* her cleavage—he changed his mind.

He could use the distraction, anyway.

Tom Nixon was standing in front of Targett's door at nine A.M. the next morning. He knocked, and heard a muffled reply from inside. When the door opened he saw Tanya standing there, naked except for a shawl she had thrown over her. There was still plenty of skin to be seen, and one brown nipple was poking through the shawl. He found himself unable to take his eyes from it.

"Hello, Tom," she said, brightly.

"Tanya," he said, "is Targett, uh, here?"

"Sure," she answered, "it's his room, isn't it?"

"Yes."

"Targett, Tom Nixon is here."

"Tell him to come in."

Nixon entered and Tanya closed the door. Targett was reclining on the bed with a sheet thrown across his loins. Tanya walked to a chair and sat down, holding the shawl around her. Sitting made it ride up her thighs, though, and Nixon even caught a flash of smooth buttocks as she sat down and brought her feet up under her.

"What can I do for you this morning?" Targett asked. "You come to tell me to get out of town?"

"Yes."

"Really?"

"Well, no," Nixon said, "actually I came to *ask* you to leave."

"On behalf of Tilghman?"

"Yes—well, no," Nixon stammered. "I mean, I'm asking you to leave so that you two won't butt heads again, but he didn't send me."

"So whose idea was it?"

"Mine, and Sheriff Sughrue."

"Well," Targett said, lacing his hands behind his head, "you know my horse is lame."

"Take another one."

"Even-up trade?"

"Even up."

"You don't have one worth my horse."

"Take two, then."

Targett studied Nixon.

"You can't be that worried about me."

"I'm not," Nixon said. "I want Bill to get off on the right foot in his new job."

"And with me here he can't?"

"For some reason," Nixon said, "you rub Bill the wrong way."

"I can't understand that," Tanya said. "Targett rubs me the right way."

To illustrate she lifted one leg, stretched it out, and ran her hands over it. The move exposed the dark hair between her legs, and a flash of moist pink. Nixon swallowed hard. He had tried to get Tanya into his bed, but had never succeeded. She was a rare breed, a choosy whore, and she had never chosen him.

When she lowered her leg he looked back at Targett. Nixon liked Targett for not having an amused smirk on his face.

"Look, Tom," Targett said, "I'll leave as soon as my horse is sound, and not before."

"And *I* hope that won't be for a long time," Tanya said. She stretched both her arms over her head and now two nipples were peeking through the shawl.

"It's only a matter of days, Tom," Targett said. "I'm sure I can stay out of Tilghman's way until then."

"I'll do my best to help him," Tanya said.

Nixon looked at Targett, and then at Tanya. He wondered if they had rehearsed this.

"All right," Nixon said, raising his hands in surrender. "I told Sughrue I'd ask, and I've asked."

"Look, Tom," Targett said, "I'll buy you lunch later and make it up to you."

"Well—"

"That way you can keep an eye on me."

"Okay," Nixon said. "One o'clock, downstairs."

"One o'clock."

Nixon took one last look at Tanya and she waved to him as he went out the door. When he was gone she laughed, leaped off the chair, threw off the shawl, and jumped on the bed with Targett.

"Well," she said, pressing her breasts tightly against his chest as she spread herself over him, "we have until one o'clock."

"To do what?"

She smiled and said, "Use your imagination."

Tom Nixon left the hotel, unhappy with himself about the way he had handled the situation. Having Tanya there, flashing skin, and nipples and . . . everything else didn't help, either.

Maybe what he should do now was talk to Tilghman about staying out of Targett's way. No, that wouldn't work. Tilghman was marshal, and as such he'd want to keep an eye—*both* eyes—on Targett.

Maybe Tanya could manage to keep Targett in his hotel room most of the time, until his horse healed. Nixon knew she would be able to keep him in *his* room for that length of time, and more.

It occurred to Nixon that he must really like Targett, because although he was envious of him being with Tanya, he didn't hold it against him.

Ten

"You want what?" Mayor Bob Wright asked.

"I want a new law passed against carrying guns within the city limits," Bill Tilghman repeated.

The two men were in the mayor's office and Wright was staring across his desk at Tilghman in disbelief.

"You can't be serious, Bill."

"I'm very serious," Tilghman said. "You heard what happened last night at the Long Branch. If no one was armed, the worst we might have had was a brawl."

"But you could never enforce such a law," Wright said. "Wearing a gun is a . . . a Western tradition."

"A bad tradition, it seems to me."

"I agree, but—"

"Mayor," Tilghman said, "give me the law and I'll enforce it."

Wright stared at Tilghman for a few moments, then shrugged and said, "I'll take it up with the council."

"When?"

"At the next meeting."

"When is that?"

"Next week. What do you—"

"Tomorrow," Tilghman said.

"Tomorrow?"

"I'd say today, but it's late in the afternoon. Tomorrow will do."

"You want me to hold a council meeting tomorrow, on a moment's notice—"

"No," Tilghman interrupted, "I want the law by tomorrow."

"That's impossible."

"I've already alerted the editor of the newspaper. He's going to run it on the front page. It'll be picked up by other newspapers. The administration in Dodge City will be considered progressive, the mayor will be considered a pioneer. Think what that would mean to you politically, Bob."

Mayor Wright did think about it and Tilghman could see that he had him.

"You'll let me know tomorrow morning?"

"I'll let you know," Mayor Wright replied. "Keep a tight rein on that editor, though. I don't want anybody jumping the gun before we're ready."

"When I get the word from you, he'll get the word from me," Tilghman said. "Thank you, Mr. Mayor."

Politicians, he though as he left; the things they'd do for a little immortality.

Over lunch Tom Nixon told Targett about what he had begun calling "Tilghman's Law."

"How will he ever enforce it?" Targett asked.

"Believe me," Nixon said, "he will."

"*If* he gets it okayed by the mayor and the town council," Targett pointed out.

"He will," Nixon said. "You don't appoint a city marshal and then ignore his requests. Besides, they have the easy part, *passing* the law. Bill's is the tough part."

"What do you think of it?"

"Well, in light of what happened last night he has a point. If no one had been armed then no one would be dead today, or wounded.

There might be some black eyes, but that would be it."

"Doesn't it take time to get a law like that passed?" Target asked.

"Bill's pushing for it tomorrow or the next day," Nixon explained.

"How is he going to manage that?"

"By appealing to the politician in Mayor Wright."

"I don't know your mayor, but it seems a sound enough strategy to take with any city official."

"It will be," Nixon said. "Wright will start seeing himself in the Governor's Mansion, and he'll exert pressure on the members of the town council to approve it. Bill already has the local newspaper ready to print the new law on page one."

"If it works," Targett said, "it will certainly put Dodge City on the map."

Nixon didn't answer. He seemed deep in thought—or deep in worry.

"What is it?" Targett questioned. "What's bothering you about it?"

Nixon pushed around the food in his plate before answering, "It might make us a target for some trouble, too."

"Well," Targett said, "it'll be just like any law. There will be the occasional odd hardcase who will try and challenge the law, but if Tilghman—*and* you—can handle that the first few times, that would pretty much put an end to it."

"It's not the first *few* times I'm worried about," Nixon said. "It's the first."

Eleven

By the next day word about what Marshal Bill Tilghman was trying to do had already gotten around. Naturally, there was some resistance.

As he breakfasted alone Targett heard the same topic of conversation at several of the tables around him:

"He's got some nerve . . ."

"Make him a marshal and look what happens . . ."

"Flexing his muscles . . ."

"Who does he think he is . . ."

"I'm not giving my gun to nobody . . ."

Of course, details would have to be worked out. People who lived in town could simply leave their guns at home when they went out. It was the people, the strangers, who rode into town who would have to have some central point at which to drop off their guns.

Targett overheard more complaints:

"Business will suffer . . ."

"Who will want to come to Dodge . . ."

"This will turn into a ghost town . . ."

"I, for one, am moving . . ."

Naturally, businessmen were worried that rather than give up their guns some men would simply bypass Dodge City in favor of another town. Targett didn't think that was likely. As long as Dodge offered the best gambling, the best food, and the best women for miles around, men would be coming here, gun law or no.

"I'm in favor of it . . . maybe it will keep our men from getting all shot up," said one woman.

Of course, the women had *their* opinions, but then they didn't carry guns . . . did they?

At that moment, over at city hall, during one of the earliest town council meetings ever held, many of the same thoughts were being verbalized.

"What are we gonna do when cowboys stop coming to town for their fun because they have to give up their guns?" asked Horace Williams, owner of the Dodge House.

"I don't think that will happen, Horace," Mayor Wright replied.

"And why not?"

"Because we'll still offer the best whiskey, food, and gambling in Kansas."

"And women," Jeff Sloan pointed out. "Don't forget women." Sloan owned the hardware store.

"We all know you'd never forget women, Jeff," Horace Williams joked and the others at the table laughed.

"Look," Mayor Wright said, "let's say we pass this law and it works, and it starts to be adopted around the country. Where did it start? Dodge. That could be important to our development."

"Whose development are we really talking about here, Bob?" Ed Samuels, owner of the town's theater asked. "Yours or the town's?"

"They're the same thing, Ed."

"How so?"

"If I go to higher office somewhere, one of you steps in as mayor. I'm talking about *all* of our growth, not just one man's. As Dodge grows, so do we all, or have we forgotten that?"

"This whole thing sounds very far-fetched," Horace Williams said.

"All right," Wright said, "let's make it a provisional law. We'll adopt it for, uh, six months, and see how it works out. If it doesn't, we'll repeal it."

"If it doesn't work," Adam Gardner said, "it will be because someone gunned down Bill Tilghman." Gardner owned the gun shop in town, and was one of the first men to suggest that Tilghman be offered the job as city marshal.

"If we go ahead and adopt this law, believe me when I say Bill Tilghman will make it work."

"All right, gentlemen," Mayor Wright said, "let's vote on this so we can get on with the day."

After all the votes were in, Mayor Wright stood up and said, "I will inform Marshal Tilghman of our decision. Have a good day, gentlemen."

Targett was seated in a chair in front of the hotel when the members of the town council filed out of the city hall. He assumed that the meeting was over and the decision had been made.

Mayor Wright had not come out, and that was probably because the marshal's office was right there in the same building.

Targett sat back and decided to enjoy his last few moments with his gun on his hip.

Bill Tilghman was in his office, even though this was Tom Nixon's shift. Nixon was in the street, making his rounds, when there was a knock on the door. "Come in," Tilghman called.

The door opened and the mayor walked in. He didn't bother to close the door.

"Well, Bill," he said, "you've got your law."

"Thank you, Mayor."

"Just do us all a favor, eh?"

"What's that?"

"Make it work."

As the mayor left and closed the door behind him Tilghman said aloud, "Oh, it will work, all right."

* * *

Targett opened his eyes and saw Tom Nixon staring down at him.

"What did I do now?" he asked.

"Nothing," Nixon said. He glanced back at the city hall.

"It's over," Targett told him.

"What?"

"The meeting," Targett said, "it's over. All the town council members have gone back to their stores for the day's business."

"And the mayor?"

"He didn't leave yet," Targett said. "Probably went right to Tilghman's office to give him the news, good or bad."

"There he is now," Nixon said, as Mayor Wright came out into the street.

They watched as the mayor walked down the street, a spring in his step.

"Looks to me like Tilghman got his law," Targett said, "and the good mayor already has visions of the governor's mansion."

"I'd better get over there," Nixon said.

"Good luck, Tom," Targett said.

"Thanks."

As Nixon went off down the street to hear the news Targett tipped his hat down over his eyes and said to no one, "You're going to need it."

Twelve

When Targett saw the afternoon edition of the *Dodge City Gazette* he figured Tilghman must have really had that editor primed and ready.

The headline screamed: *NO GUNS IN DODGE!*

The article went on to explain that no one but law officers would be allowed to carry firearms within the city limits. It further stated that strangers would be greeted by Marshal Bill Tilghman and informed that they would have to drop their guns off at Wright's General Store on their way *into* town, where they could pick them up on their way *out* of town. The article ended by saying that the law would go into effect tomorrow morning.

In an editorial the newspaper lauded both Marshal Bill Tilghman and Mayor Bob Wright for coming up with this law, and the town council for approving it.

Targett put the newspaper down on the other side of the table and proceeded with his lunch. He wondered if Tilghman had agreed to share the credit for the concept of the law with the mayor, or if that was the mayor's idea entirely. Either way, there wasn't much Tilghman would be able to do about it now that it was in print.

Targett was very interested in seeing what the streets of Dodge City would look like in the morning.

"Did you know about this?" Tom Nixon asked.

He was seated on Tilghman's desk, as they still did not have a second chair. The office was, however, spotless, thanks to the efforts of Flora Tilghman, so Nixon was able to rest his buttocks on the desk without fear of picking up a pound of dust.

"What?"

"Wright's taking part of the credit for coming up with this law."

Tilghman waved that away.

"I don't care who gets credit for coming up with it as long as I got the law passed."

Tilghman was busy writing something down on a piece of paper.

"Well, it burns me, I can tell you. Would you vote for him if he ran for governor?"

"That would depend on who he was running against."

"You're too forgiving," Nixon said, throwing the paper down.

"I have nothing to forgive," Tilghman said. "He gave me what *I* wanted, so I have no objection to him getting what *he* wants."

"All right, forget about Wright," Nixon said. "How are we going to work this?"

"Like this," Tilghman said, turning the piece of paper he had been writing on so that Nixon could read it.

"You want me to read this to anyone who rides into town?" Nixon asked, pointing at the note.

"Put it in your own words if you want, but that's the message I want to get across."

Tilghman wanted strangers informed that there was a new law in Dodge against carrying guns, and that the law was to not only to prevent them from shooting anyone, but to prevent them from being shot, themselves. Strangers would be informed that if anyone cheated them at cards or watered their whiskey they were to come to Tilghman or to his deputy and the law would take care of it.

"Just end by saying 'Welcome to Dodge City, and have a good time'" Tilghman added.

"Do you think they'll believe we mean that?" Nixon queried.

"I'll mean it," Tilghman said. "Imagine how much of a good time people can have when they don't have to be afraid that they're going to be shot."

"Look at the other side of the coin," Nixon said.

"What do you mean?"

"How many card cheats will come to town to ply their trade because they can't be shot?"

"Maybe they can't be shot at the table, but they can be brought to justice," Tilghman said, "by us, and that's the whole point."

"I suppose."

Tilghman looked at Nixon and said, "Tom, are you going to be one of those people who doesn't agree with me on this?"

"Let's put it this way, Bill," Nixon said. "I'll be just like everybody else. If it works I'll agree with you, if it doesn't . . ."

"Well, at least you're honest."

"There's one other thing, though."

"What's that?"

"You asked me to be your deputy, so no matter what I think, this is now a law, and I'll uphold it as long as it *is* a law."

"I know you will," Tilghman said. "That's why I asked you to be my deputy."

Tilghman sat back in his chair and rubbed his hands over his face.

"What the hell time is it?" he asked. "Whose shift it is?"

"It's not yet three," Nixon said, "but why don't you go on home? I'll work a little overtime."

Tilghman nodded and said, "Flora will be glad to see me . . . I think."

"Speaking of Flora, she did a wonderful job on the office, but who's gonna keep it clean?"

Tilghman stood up and said, "That reminds *me*. Buy a broom at Wright's today."

"And?"

Tilghman went to the door, then turned and said smiling, "Use it."

Thirteen

That night the new law was the topic of conversation at the Long Branch.

"It's totally ridiculous," a man at the bar said.

"Why?" another asked.

"How are we supposed to defend ourselves?"

"Against what?"

"Against someone with a gun."

"But no one is allowed to wear a gun," the second man said, "so why do we need a gun to protect us from someone without a gun?"

"Huh?" the first man said.

"I don't know," the second man said. "I just confused myself."

Targett was standing at the end of the bar tonight, rather than sitting at a table.

"What do you think of the new law?" the bartender asked him when serving him his second beer.

"I think anyone who doesn't like it can go somewhere else," Targett said. "If you're going to live in a town, you abide by its laws. If you're going to visit a town, you abide by its laws."

"You sound like a pretty law abiding citizen," the barman said.

Targett sipped his beer and said, "Whenever it suits my needs."

"I wonder how technical Tilghman's going to be?" the bartender said.

"What do you mean?"

"Well, it's almost midnight," the man said, "and there are a lot of men in here wearing guns, including yourself. The newspaper didn't say what *time* in the morning the law would go into effect."

"I don't think even Bill Tilghman would walk in here tonight and take everybody's guns," Targett said. "For one thing, he wouldn't be able to carry them all."

At that point Bill Tilghman walked into the saloon, followed by a man who was carrying something underneath his arm. It was very long and made of wood.

Tilghman went to the wall next to the batwing doors, removed a picture that was hanging there, and then turned and said something to the other man.

"Excuse me," the bartender said. He left the bar and went to a door at the back of the room, which Targett assumed was the office of the owner.

Tilghman and the other man proceeded to nail this wooden thing to the wall, and Targett could see that there were many wooden pegs sticking out from it. Once it was on, he could see that it was a long pegboard, and it wasn't hard to figure out what was supposed to hang on those pegs.

"Can I have your attention, please?" Tilghman shouted.

The door in the back wall opened and the bartender came out, followed by another man.

"Attention . . . please!" Tilghman called again.

Everyone in the room fell silent and the owner quickly crossed the crowded room.

"Tilghman, what are you—"

"In a minute, Clark," Tilghman said, brushing the man off.

Tilghman turned back to the crowded room and made his announcement.

"It is now after midnight, which means it is tomorrow morning.

Anyone wishing to stay here in the Long Branch beyond this point will either have to go home and leave his gun, or hang the gunbelt up right here until you leave. This is all in compliance with Dodge City's new gun law."

"This is ridiculous," the owner of the Long Branch said. "You can't put a thing like that on my wall."

"It is absolutely necessary that I *do* put such a thing on your wall, Clark." He turned to the room again and said, "I want to see some gunbelts hanging from there."

Clark turned to the room and frowned and none of his customers made any move to comply.

"I guess it wasn't made clear in the newspaper that there would be fines or prison sentences imposed for anyone who does not comply."

Apparently the owner of the Long Branch, Clark, exerted some influence over his customers. Targett could feel the tension in the air as Tilghman and Clark faced each other, and everyone in the room was waiting to see who would blink first. To make his stand even clearer Clark put his hands on his hip and in doing so brushed back his jacket to reveal a gun in a shoulder rig.

Targett put down his beer and walked across the floor. He could feel all eyes on him as he unbuckled his gunbelt, hung it on a peg, then walked back to the bar and picked up his beer.

Clark had turned to follow his progress back to the bar and Targett acknowledged his gaze by raising his beer mug to him.

Now that Targett had broken the ice, two men sitting at one table together stood up, removed their gunbelts and hung them on pegs. Behind them came another man, then three, then six and then a dozen—and then a line formed as men waited to hang up their guns.

With the stalemate broken Clark turned and stalked back across the room, closing his office door behind him with a bang.

Tilghman watched as the men hung up their guns, and occasionally looked over at Targett, who was still standing at the bar. The bartender had returned to his place behind the bar.

* * *

Of course, there were those who would have to challenge Tilghman. The Marshal knew that, and he was ready to do what was necessary to convince everyone—*everyone!*—that he meant business.

Four men seated at a corner table were very much the center of attention, because none of the four had given up therir guns. Targett was now sorry that he had given up his. If Tilghman and the other man had to go against these four men, they would have no backup.

Silently, with a wave of his hand, Targett called the bartender over.

"What have you got behind the bar?"

The bartender knew what he meant.

"An ax handle, and a shotgun."

The four men were too far away for the ax handle to be of any use.

"Slide the shotgun over here where I can reach it."

The bartender nodded and did as he was told, then moved away from Targett—as far away as he could get.

Now all eyes were on Tilghman as he approached the table where the four armed men sat. The other man positioned himself slightly behind Tilghman, but to his left. He was holding a rifle in his hands.

"You gents don't seem to have heard me."

One of the men looked up at Tilghman and said, "We heard you."

The four men were of a kind, in their thirties, worn trail clothes and hard looks. This man seemed to be their spokesman.

"I take it that means you refuse to give up your guns?" Tilghman said.

"You got that right, Marshal," the man said. "Me and my friends came into your town for a meal, a drink and a place to sleep. We'll be on our way in the mornin'."

"Do you fellas plan on turning in now?"

"No," the man said, "we got some more drinkin' to do before we turn in."

"Then you will kindly put your guns on that board over there."

The man seemed on the verge of losing his patience.

"I tole you, Marshal—" he started, but Tilghman did not allow him to get any further in his statement. The Marshal took a step forward and dug into the man's right armpit with his left hand. Holding him that way he lifted the larger man to his feet with surprising strength and relieved him of his gun with his right hand.

"Hey!" the man said, and swung his left fist at Tilghman.

Tilghman blocked the blow with his right arm, then hit the man in the face with his elbow. He could have used the man's gun on him, because it was still in his hand, but he opted for the elbow, and the effect was just as good. The man's nose exploded into a shower of red and he staggered back.

The other three men all rose and went for their guns.

"Don't!" Tilghman's man shouted, pointing his rifle, but he wouldn't be able to shoot all three men, if it came to that.

Just as Tilghman lifted the man from his seat, Targett had reached and come out from behind the bar with the shotgun.

"I'd listen to the man if I was you, gents!" he shouted loudly.

The three men, now covered by a rifle and a shotgun, subsided, but their shoulders and arms were still tense.

"All right," Tilghman said. "Glover, get their guns."

The man with the rifle moved to each man in turn and relieved them of their guns.

Tilghman took this opportunity to turn to the room and say, "Let this be a lesson. There will be no exceptions to this law!"

Once all the guns in the place were hanging on pegs Tilghman instructed the other man, Glover, to take a chair and sit by the guns. It became obvious that Tilghman had deputized the man to sit by the guns with a rifle across his lap.

"When you are ready to leave Mr. Glover here will allow you to take your guns. I would advise you then to go indoors. Any man observed carrying a gun on the street will be stopped by me."

Targett was sure that after today that peg board would hardly be used because guns would already have been given up by the time men got to the saloons. This was simply a statement that Tilghman was making, as if to say, "Yes, this *is* a law I *will* enforce it."

In Targett's opinion, Tilghman had made his point admirably.

"All right, you fellas," Tilghman said to the three now unarmed men, "pick up your friend and let's go. You'll be spending the night in jail."

"We was leavin' in the mornin'," one of the men grumbled while the other two helped the bloodied man to his feet.

"Don't worry," Tilghman said, "I'll let you out in plenty of time to get an early start."

By now Targett had returned the shotgun to the bartender. As Tilghman marched the men to the batwing doors he looked over at Targett and gave him an almost inperceptible nod of thanks.

Inperceptible, that is, to everyone but Targett, who appreciated the gesture.

Fourteen

Targett woke the next morning when the sunlight streaming through the window fell across his face. Tanya was lying on his left arm, her breath warm against the nape of his neck. He slid his arm from beneath her without waking her and slipped from the bed. He walked naked to the window and stood directly in front of it, looking out. It was too early for the street to be busy, but the two men he did see were not wearing guns.

"What is it?" Tanya asked from behind him. "What do you see?"

"Nothing."

He turned and looked at her. She had propped herself up on her right elbow, and the sheet had fallen away from her, exposing her breasts.

"There must be something out there," she said, "something that took you away from me and over to the window."

He shook his head and said, "Nothing."

"Then come back to bed," she said. "I'm cold."

He walked back to the bed and slid in beside her. She pressed herself against him and put her head on his shoulder. She was wrong—she wasn't cold, she was burning up. She had by far the warmest skin of any woman he'd ever known.

He stroked her back with his hand and she was asleep in moments.

He couldn't tell her what had taken him from the bed to the window, because he wasn't quite sure himself. It was a sudden sense of . . . what? Foreboding?

Something was in the wind, and if his horse was healed enough he could leave Dodge before it got there.

But did he want to?

"I thought the town council only approved a budget for marshal and *one* deputy," Tom Nixon said.

Tilghman had come to the office early, during Nixon's shift, because he wanted to be around when the streets started filling up with people.

"They did."

"Where did you get the money to hire Glover?"

Tilghman didn't answer.

"You used your own money?" Nixon asked, aghast.

"It was only for one night."

"To make a point."

"Right."

"And did you make it?"

"Thanks to your friend, yes."

"My friend?"

"Targett."

"Targett? What did he have to do with it?"

"He was the first one to hang up his gun," Tilghman said. "If he hadn't started it off I think I might have had some problems."

"With who?"

"Dan Clark."

"What was his problem?"

"He didn't like me putting holes in his wall."

Tilghman explained how Clark had stood up to him, and by doing so had almost bullied everyone into doing so—until Targett changed things.

"Targett," Nixon said. "Why do you suppose he did it?"

"I don't know," Tilghman said. "Maybe you could ask him."

Nixon hesitated before asking the next question. "Why don't you?"

Tilghman made a face and didn't reply—and he didn't look up at Nixon.

"Because you might have to thank him?" Nixon said, prodding him.

"For what?" Tilghman said. "He obeyed the law. Am I to thank a man for that?"

"You're a stubborn cuss, Bill Tilghman," Nixon said, shaking his head.

Tilghman stood up. "Let's go and spend some time on the street."

"Checking hips?"

"If anyone shows up on the street with a gun I want him locked up, Tom," Tilghman said. "If you don't think you can do that—"

"I'll do it, don't worry," Nixon said, interrupting Tilghman.

"Thanks, Tom."

"For what?" Nixon asked. "I'll just be upholding the law." He walked to the door and said, "Why should you thank a man for that?"

Nixon closed the door behind him, leaving Tilghman to stare at it.

Stubborn? That was what Flora said, also.

Fifteen

Targett had an early breakfast in the hotel dining room with Tanya. She drew some disapproving looks from some of the townswomen who were eating there. Obviously, they were wondering what right a whore had to have breakfast in the same place they did.

Targett and Tanya made a point of acknowledging every dirty look they got with a smile.

"I love this," Tanya said, "rubbing their faces in it. They don't like me eating where they eat, but how many of them have taken their husbands to their bed straight from mine?"

Targett had to admit she had a good point there.

After breakfast Tanya went to her room upstairs from the Long Branch and Targett sat himself down in front of the hotel, where he would be able to view all of the festivities.

At 9:30 A.M. the first man was arrested for carrying a gun in Dodge City. Bill Tilghman took him in and put him in a cell at the sheriff's office. The man explained that he had been away from Dodge for two weeks and had just returned. Therefore, he was unaware of the new law.

He was released.

At 10:05 A.M. Tom Nixon arrested a man who refused to remove his gunbelt when told to. When the man was behind bars in the sheriff's office he cried out that Dan Clark would pay his fine.

"Will he serve your time?" Nixon asked, and left the man to ponder that thought.

By noon, five men in all had been arrested and it became clear that at least three of them had been put up to wearing their guns and refusing to remove them by Dan Clark, the owner of the Long Branch.

Bill Tilghman walked into the Long Branch at two p.m. and approached the bar. There were about six people in the saloon and they all stopped to watch him.

"W-what can I do for you, Marshal?" the bartender asked.

"I want to see your boss."

"Uh, the boss is asleep right now—"

"Wake him up," Tilghman said.

The man laughed nervously.

"I can't do that, Marshal. You don't know how mad he gets when—"

"I don't *care* how mad he gets," Tilghman interrupted. "You wake him up or I will."

"All right, all right," the bartender said. He obviously felt that Clark would be even more upset if Tilghman woke him.

"Can I give you a drink while you're waiting?"

"No."

"O-okay," the man said. "I'll go upstairs and wake him."

"Tell him that if he doesn't come down here to see me, I'll come up to see him."

"I'll tell him."

Tilghman watched as the bartender walked upstairs, and then turned to look at the other men in the saloon. He stared at them until two of them stood up and carefully left the saloon, holding their arms away from their bodies to make sure that the marshal saw they were not wearing guns.

That left four men for Tilghman to watch, and from his vantage point he could see that three of them were not armed.

The fourth man sat at the back of the room with a beer, and Tilghman noticed that he was a stranger. He wondered when he had ridden into town, and how he had done so with neither he himself nor Nixon seeing him.

Tilghman pushed away from the bar and walked to the man's table.

"Excuse me," Tilghman said.

The man looked up and said, "Are you talking to me, Marshal?"

"I am," Tilghman said. "You're a stranger in town."

The man smiled, and it was not a pleasant smile.

"You know that for sure, huh? You know everyone in town real well?"

"Well enough," Tilghman said. "I wonder if you know of our no-gun-law here in Dodge City?"

"No gun?"

"No one but a lawman is permitted to carry a gun in Dodge."

"Well, that's a right nice law, Marshal . . . for you," the man said.

Tilghman studied the stranger. He was in his thirties, not a pleasant-looking man by any means. Tilghman guessed the man would be about six feet standing up.

"What's your name?"

"Valentine," the man replied, "Greg Valentine."

"When did you arrive in town?"

"Oh, I've been here quite some time."

"How long is that?"

The man shrugged and was saved from having to answer by the appearance of the bartender.

"Marshal—" the bartender said.

"Just a minute," Tilghman said. "Mr. Valentine, are you wearing a gun?"

As an answer Valentine pointed beyond Tilghman towards the front wall. Tilghman turned and saw a gun and holster hanging on the pegboard. The gun was a nickel-plated, pearl-handled forty-five.

"That's your gun?" Tilghman asked, with a slight smile on his face.

"It is," Valentine said, his tone somewhat wounded. "What's wrong with it?"

"Nothing," Tilghman said, "it's very pretty." He turned to the bartender and said, "So, where is your boss?"

"Uh, he asked me to let you into his office and said he would be with you in a few minutes."

"Well, then, let's go."

The bartender led the way to the door in the back and let Tilghman in.

"He told me to offer you a drink."

Tilghman just stared at the bartender.

"Right," the man said, and backed out of the room.

Sixteen

When Targett saw Tom Nixon crossing the street toward him he stood up, moved his hands away from his body, turned once completely around, and then sat himself back down again.

"Give me a break," Nixon said. He sat down on the boardwalk at Targett's feet.

"Rough day?"

"Five arrests," Nixon said, "and only one was out of ignorance of the new law."

"And the others?"

"Put up to it by Dan Clark," Nixon said. "Three of them for sure, but the fourth one, too, I'll bet."

"Clark's trying to bust the law on the first day."

"He's not going to do it," Nixon said. "Tilghman's gone over to confront him."

"Alone?"

Nixon stared at Targett for a moment, then said, "No, not alone," and stood up and headed for the Long Branch.

After a moment Targett got up and followed him.

Just out of curiosity.

*   *   *

Tilghman figured Valentine for a gun hired by Dan Clark—but to do what? He hadn't had time to send for him in response to the new gun law. He must have sent for him before that.

Why?

The office door opened and Dan Clark came in, looking as dapper as ever. He didn't look like a man who had been abruptly awakened.

"What's so important that you had to wake me, Tilghman?"

"You don't look like you just woke up."

"You do," Clark said, moving around behind his desk. He seated himself and said, "Well?"

"I want you to call off your men," Tilghman said. "I don't have enough jail cells for them."

Clark stared at Tilghman. "You're really doing it, aren't you?"

"Does that surprise you?" Tilghman responded, gazing evenly at Clark.

"Frankly," Clark said, "yes. I thought when you realized how ridiculous this whole thing was you'd call it off."

"Maybe I will," Tilghman said, standing up, "*when* I realize how ridiculous it all is. For now, stop interfering with the performance of my job. The next one of your men I jail, you'll be right with him."

"You can't—"

"Yes," Tilghman said, "I can . . . and I will."

Tilghman opened the door and left.

Nixon entered the Long Branch and looked around for Tilghman. All he saw were four men seated at tables, and the bartender behind the bar.

"Hello, Tom," the bartender said. "Beer?"

"Sure, Fred."

"For your friend, too?"

"My friend?" Nixon asked, frowning. He looked behind him and saw that Targett had entered. "Yeah, give him one, too."

"Thanks," Targett said.

He walked past Nixon to the bar, and at the same time caught a glimpse of the gun hanging on the pegboard.

He went to the bar and picked up his beer, then looked at all four of the other men in the room, through the mirror behind the bar. His eyes finally fell on the man sitting in the back.

Nixon appeared next to him and picked up his beer.

"Where's the marshal, Fred?" Nixon asked the bartender.

"In the office with the boss. What's going on, anyway, Tom?"

"Your boss and my boss are buttin' heads."

"Again?"

Nixon nodded.

"Something's gotta give some time, Tom. Can't you do something about Tilghman?"

Nixon put down his beer and said, "Can't you do something about Clark?"

"I don't have any influence with him," Fred said. "You do, with the marshal."

"I'm starting to wonder."

The door to the office opened and Tilghman stepped out. Fred, Nixon, and Targett all turned to look. Tilghman frowned and approached the bar.

"What are you doing here?" he asked Nixon.

Nixon shrugged and said, "Thought you might need some help."

"Good thought," Tilghman said, "but not necessary."

"What went on in there?"

"I don't think we'll have any more trouble today," Tilghman said. "At least not from any of Clark's men. We'd better get back out on the street."

"Right," Nixon said. "Thanks for the beer, Fred."

Nixon left without looking at Targett. Tilghman, however, turned and looked directly at Targett.

"And what are you doing here?"

Targett lifted his mug and said, "I just came in for a drink."

"How is your horse doing?"

"Coming along," Targett said. "Should be another couple of days."

Tilghman nodded, then just turned and left.

"I don't think he likes you," Fred said.

"I guess not."

"That may make you pretty popular around here."

"Oh yeah?" Targett said. "With who?"

"My boss."

"Even after last night?"

Fred shrugged.

"Maybe because of last night. You showed some real guts."

"You think so, huh?"

"Want me to talk to him for you?"

Targett waited a moment, as if he was thinking it over real well, and then said, "No, I don't think so."

Fred frowned and said, "Why not?"

Targett shrugged.

"What would I do?"

"You a fair hand with a gun?"

Targett shook his head.

"Terrible."

"Come on . . ."

"Besides," Targett said, "Clark doesn't need my gun, he's already got himself one. A real pretty gun, too." Targett turned his head to look at the pearl-handled gun on the pegboard.

The bartender looked over at the gun also, and then smiled dreamily.

"It's a nice piece, isn't it?" Fred said. "Wish I could afford me a gun like that."

"Yeah, it's real fancy, all right," Targett said, "but that doesn't mean it can shoot any straighter than any other gun. That little detail is completely up to the man holding it."

"Oh, that ain't no problem," Fred said.

He leaned forward as if he were about to impart an important secret.

"You know whose gun that is?"

"Yeah, I do," Targett said. He looked in the mirror at the man sitting at the back table and said, "Mr. Valentine's."

Seventeen

Targett finished his beer and left the empty mug on the bar. He turned and walked over to the pegboard and slid the gun out of the holster. When Fred saw him do that he caught his breath.

"Don't touch that gun!" the gun's owner ordered.

Targett turned and looked at Valentine. The man hadn't moved an inch.

"What?"

"Put it back."

Targett examined the gun in his hand for a moment.

"I was just taking a look at it."

"Now that you've taken a look at it, put it back," Valentine said.

Targett looked at Valentine again, held his gaze, then shrugged and put the gun back.

"I wouldn't have any use for a fancy piece like that, anyway," he said aloud.

"Is that a fact?"

"It's too pretty," Targett said. "Who would want to kill a man with something that pretty?"

"It's been known to happen."

"I know," Targett said.

Valentine was studying him now, as if he knew him from somewhere.

"St. Louis," Targett said to help him, "about four years ago."

Recognition dawned on Valentine's face.

"Targett, isn't it?"

"It is."

"Well I'll be damned," Valentine said. "Fred, give the man another beer on me. Bring it on over here and drink it, Targett."

"Sure," Targett said, "sure, Valentine. Who am I to turn down a free beer?"

"And bring me one, while you're at it."

Targett picked up two beers and carried them over to Valentine's table.

"So, what have you been doing for the past four years?" Valentine asked.

"My job."

"Still helpin' people find stuff they lost?"

"I don't do it for nothing," Targett said, "just like you don't do what you do for nothing."

"Why would I do it for nothing?" Valentine asked. "I don't even like it."

Targett doubted that. You don't kill with a gun like Valentine's without some enjoyment, he thought.

"What brings you to Dodge?" Valentine asked.

"Passing through."

"On your way to where?"

"Back to San Francisco."

"Back home, huh?"

"That's right," Targett said. "What are you doing here?"

"I work for Clark."

"Doing what?"

Valentine grinned, his manner cocky. "Doing what I do best."

"Which you don't enjoy."

"Of course not."

"Who's your target?"

Valentine gave Targett a narrowed-eyed look.

"Why do you want to know?"

"Hey, Valentine," Targett said, "we're just a couple of guys making conversation. Remember, *you* asked *me* to come over and sit. If you don't want to talk . . ." Targett said, starting to get up.

"Hey, hold it," Valentine said. "Don't be so sensitive."

Targett sat back down.

"I've been here for three days, under wraps, with nobody to talk to but some uneducated yahoos with shit on their boots," Valentine complained.

"Three days?"

"Yeah, sitting upstairs. The only time I enjoy myself is when they send me one of the girls." He leaned forward and said, "They got this gal named Lisa, with an *incredible* body—"

"I know about Lisa," Targett said.

"Yeah," Valentine said, "I guess it would be kind of hard to keep a gal like that a secret."

"So how much longer will you be here?"

"I don't rightly know," Valentine answered. "Mr. Clark is paying me enough to hang around and wait until he needs me, so that's what I'll do. May not be so bad now that I've got somebody to talk to, huh? I got to go back to my hole before the saloon fills up. Why don't you come up and play some two-handed poker? Or else we'll have Lisa and another gal come up."

"I'll see if I can make it, Valentine," Targett said. "I'm waiting for my lame horse to heal so I can move out. In fact, I've got to check on him now."

"Well, just tell Fred there if you want to come up and he'll let you by."

"What if Clark finds out?"

"If he wants me to stay here bad enough he won't be saying nothing."

The door to the office opened just then and Clark stepped out. When he saw Targett and Valentine sitting together his face turned red and he stormed over.

"What the hell are you doing down here?" he demanded, facing Valentine.

"I got lonely upstairs, Clark," Valentine retorted. "I thought I'd come down and get a drink or two. I met an old friend. Do you know Targett?"

Clark looked at Targett and said, "We've met." He looked back at Valentine and said, "I thought I told you I didn't want to see you down here. Did Tilghman see you?"

"We had a nice talk, and I showed him my gun hanging on the board over there."

"Jesus," Clark said. "Get your gun and go back upstairs, Valentine. I'll be up to talk to you in a few minutes."

Valentine hesitated just a moment, then shrugged and said, "It's your money, so you're the boss." Valentine looked at Targett and said, "Remember what I said."

"Sure."

Valentine stood up, retrieved his gun, slung the belt over his shoulder, and went upstairs.

"What are you doing here?" Clark demanded of Targett.

"I came in for a drink and met an old friend. Seeing Valentine here makes me wonder what you need a hired killer for, Clark."

"I'm an important man in this town, Targett," Clark said. "I need protection."

"From who?"

"From those who would do me harm."

"Like Tilghman?"

Clark grinned wolfishly. "Are you trying to get me to admit that I hired a killer to come to town and take care of Marshal Bill Tilghman?"

"Not at all," Targett replied, standing up. He was several inches taller than Clark. "Even if you did it would be no skin off my nose."

"Is that so?" Clark said. "You're something of a mystery, aren't you, Targett?"

"I don't think so."

Clark folded his arms across his chest and studied Targett critically.

"I do. I hear you don't get along with Tilghman, yet you helped him out last night."

"The way I look at it, Clark," Targett said, "I helped *you* out last night."

Clark frowned.

"How do you figure that?"

"I kept you out of jail, Clark," Targett said. He headed for the door, then turned and said, "Think about it."

Eighteen

When Targett left the saloon he went to the town hall to the marshal's office to look for Tilghman or Nixon. Neither one was there, so he went to the sheriff's office.

Pat Sughrue looked up when Targett entered.

"Well, I'm glad you're not wearing a gun."

"Why?"

"Because I don't have any more room in my jail, that's why. What can I do for you, Targett?"

"I'm looking for the marshal."

"Well, he's not here."

"I can see that," Targett said. "Can you tell me where I can find him?"

"How should I know. He's probably out arresting more people for having guns."

"What about Nixon, the deputy?"

"Him, too."

"No, I mean do you know where he is?"

"No."

"All right," Targett said. It was plain that the sheriff was not in the mood for visitors.

"Wait a minute," Sughrue said as Targett went to the door.

"What?"

"Aren't you supposed to be staying out of Tilghman's way?"

"I am," Targett said, "but there's something he should know."

"What?"

"I'll tell him, and then let him tell you."

"Sure," Sughrue said, "hire a marshal and the sheriff becomes a second-class citizen."

Targett decided to leave before the sheriff picked his shoulder to cry on.

Targett walked around town until he finally found Tom Nixon.

"Where have you been hiding?" Targett asked.

"Who's hiding?" Nixon said. "I'm making my rounds looking for illegal guns."

"Where is Tilghman?"

"He should be around, why?"

"I've got something to tell him."

"Targett, do me a favor," Nixon said, "stay away from Tilghman."

"There's something he should know, Tom."

"Like what?"

"Did you see the gun that was hanging on the wall at the Long Branch?"

"What gun?"

"The nickel-plated, pearl-handled forty-five."

"No, I didn't see it, why?"

"Because I recognized it, that's why, and the man it belongs to."

"Who?" Nixon said. "Who is he?"

"His name is Valentine."

"Valentine?" Nixon said. "He doesn't sound very dangerous— and he carries a pearl-handled gun? Is this a joke?"

"Believe me, Tom," Targett said, "Valentine is no joke. He's very good at what he does for a living."

"Which is?"

"He kills people."

"And who is he here to kill?"

"I don't know," Targett said, "but he's working for Clark."

"Jesus," Nixon said, "he must be here for Tilghman."

"Maybe," Targett said, "but whether he is or isn't Tilghman should be told."

"Let's check the other side of town," Nixon said. "He's got to be over there, somewhere."

"What about his house?"

"It's on that side of town," Nixon said. "Maybe he went home for something to eat."

Together they started walking towards Tilghman's house.

"Tell me something," Nixon said.

"What?"

"How did you get this information?"

"I talked to Valentine."

"Why would he talk to you?"

"We've met before."

"Where?"

"In St. Louis, four years ago. We were both there doing a job and our paths intersected."

"Anything happen?"

"No," Targett said. "Valentine wasn't being paid to kill me, and he doesn't do it for free."

"Don't tell me he's got ethics."

"Why not? Just because he's a killer doesn't mean he can't have ethics."

"I'll never understand that."

They walked a bit further before Nixon asked, "What were you doing in St. Louis?"

"Working."

When Targett didn't elaborate Nixon said, "Let me ask you a question you can answer."

"Like what?"

"Why are you doing this?"

"Doing what?"

"Warning Tilghman," Nixon said. "Standing up for him last night?"

"I thought you said you were going to ask me a question I could answer."

"You can't answer," Nixon said, "or you won't?"

Targett was quiet for a moment and then he said, "I'm here, Tom. I'm not just going to stand around while people get killed over some silly new law."

"You think it's silly?"

"Of course it's silly," Targett said. "Carrying a gun is a man's right, and any law that takes that away is just *plain* silly."

"Would you tell that to Tilghman?"

"I would," Targett said, "but I don't think he'd ever ask me. I don't imagine my opinion means much to him."

"Maybe not," Nixon said, "but he'll have to take this information seriously."

Targett put his hand on Nixon's arm to stop him.

"You have a good point," Targett said. "If he knows this information came from me is he stubborn enough to ignore it?"

"He's *just* stubborn enough to ignore it."

"All right," Targett said. "I'm going to go check on my horse. You go find Tilghman and tell him *you* found out about Valentine."

"From who?"

Targett looked at the man and said, "Use your imagination, Tom."

Nineteen

Tilghman was having lunch with his wife when there was a knock on the kitchen door. Flora Tilghman got up and let Tom Nixon in.

"Can I get you a cup of coffee, Tom?"

"Yes, Flora, thanks."

"Some lunch?"

"No, just coffee, thanks."

Nixon sat at the table with Tilghman, who was lunching on cold meatloaf. Flora placed a cup of coffee in front of him and the two men looked at each other across the table.

"All right," Flora Tilghman said, "I'll leave you gentlemen to your business."

As she left the kitchen Tilghman said, "What brings you here?"

"Information."

"On what?"

"Clark's brought in a hired killer."

Tilghman stopped eating and stared at Nixon.

"The pearl handle?"

"You saw him?"

"I spoke to him," Tilghman said, putting down his fork, "but I was interrupted."

"Maybe we should talk to him again?" Nixon queried.

"Yeah, why not." Tilghman said. He picked up his fork and added, "After lunch."

"Sure," Nixon said, "but we'll have to locate him. Clark is not going to parade this guy around town."

"Good point," Tilghman said, "but tell me something."

"What?"

"Where did you get all this information?"

"Uh, I got it . . . around."

"Around where?"

"From . . ."

"Targett?"

Nixon looked down into his cup.

"Tom, do you *like* this man, Targett?"

"Yes, I do," Nixon said, defensively. "I don't think he's the way *you* think he is."

"What do *I* think?" Tilghman prodded.

"That he's a killer."

"I never said that."

"No, but you treat him that way, and he hasn't done anything to deserve it."

"His record—"

"So he bends the law a little," Nixon said. "He hasn't done it while he's been in Dodge. How about judging him by what you see rather than what you've heard or read?"

A muscle in Tilghman's jaw began to twitch.

"Why don't you see if you can locate this Valentine while I finish my lunch?" he replied. "I'll meet you in front of the Long Branch in half an hour."

"Fine," Nixon said, standing up. "Tell Flora thanks for the coffee."

As Nixon stormed out Tilghman set his fork down again. His feelings about Targett and his kind were starting to affect his relationship with Nixon.

Maybe it had been a mistake to take a friend as a deputy.

As Nixon walked to the Long Branch he wondered if he had made a mistake taking the job as Tilghman's deputy. He just didn't have the same attitude towards the law that the marshal did. Was that always going to make for problems between them?

Nixon would rather turn in his badge than lose Tilghman as a friend.

After Targett left Nixon he went to the livery to check on his horse.

"Hello, young fella," the liveryman said. "Come to see about your horse?"

"Yes."

"Well, come and take a look."

He followed the old man to the horse's stall.

"Good as new," the man said.

Targett leaned over and ran his hand up and down the horse's leg. The swelling was gone, and so was the heat. The horse was sound.

"I took the wrap off this morning," the old man said.

Targett stood up straight and said, "Put it back on this afternoon."

The old man stared at Targett for a moment, as if he hadn't understood what was said.

"What?"

"I said put the wrap back on," Targett said.

"Why? He's fine."

"Because I say so," Targett said. He took out a couple of dollars and said, "Have dinner on me tonight—and keep this just between us."

"Okay," the man said, taking the money, "but how long does the wrap stay on?"

"Until I tell you to take it off," Targett said. "Got it?"

"I got it, mister," the man said, tucking the money away in his shirt pocket. "I don't understand it, but I got it."

"Good," Targett said, "and remember—this is just between us."

"I said I got it."

"Don't even tell the deputy. Understand?"

"I may be old, sonny," the man said, "but I ain't senile. If I *say* I got it, I got it."

Targett left the livery, not even sure himself why he was doing what he was doing. To leave now, he figured, was sort of like going to a theater to see a show, and then walking out in the middle.

This was one show he knew he didn't want to miss the end of.

Twenty

When Tom Nixon entered the Long Branch it was considerably busier than it had been before. He looked at the pegboard on the wall and saw that it was empty. He went to the bar and ordered a beer.

When the bartender brought it over he said, "Fred, that pearl-handled gun that was on the wall earlier today."

"Yeah, what about it?"

"Where is the owner?"

"The owner, Tom?"

"Come on, Fred, don't let the badge fool you," Tom said, even though he didn't even *have* a badge yet. "It's still me, Tom Nixon. The man's name is Valentine. Where is he staying?"

Fred looked around nervously, to see if anyone was close enough to hear him, before answering.

"He's staying upstairs, Tom," Fred said.

"Is he up there now?"

"Yeah," Fred said, "with Lisa."

"Okay," Tom said. "I'm gonna sit at a table and nurse this."

"Tom, is there gonna be trouble?"

"No trouble, Fred," Nixon said. "Not so long as everyone cooperates."

Fred nervously glanced at the door of Dan Clark's office.

"That's fine, Fred," Nixon said, reading his thoughts. "I don't want you to get into trouble either. You can tell Clark I was asking."

"I gotta think of my job, Tom," Fred said, apologetically.

"I know, Fred," Nixon said. "We all have the same problem. Uh, when you talk to Clark just tell him not to move Valentine. It wouldn't be advisable."

"I'll tell him."

Tom Nixon went to a table in the back—by coincidence, the same table Valentine had been sitting at earlier in the day—and sat down to wait for Tilghman.

Fred went to the office to talk to Clark.

For want of something else to do Targett went from the livery to the Long Branch. When he saw Nixon sitting at a table he got a beer from Fred and went to join him.

"Busy?" he asked.

"Waiting," Nixon said.

"For what, or who?"

"For the marshal."

Targett, who was in the act of sitting, straightened up again and said, "I'd better sit somewhere else."

"I'm supposed to meet him out front in"—Nixon checked his watch—"fifteen minutes."

Targett sat down.

"I wouldn't want to get you fired."

"If he fires me because of you then my job was never that secure in the first place."

"What are you two up to?"

"We're gonna talk to Valentine."

"How did the marshal take the news?"

"He took it well," Nixon said, "but he didn't like where I got it."

"You told him?"

Nixon shrugged.

"What can I say? I guess I don't have much of an imagination."

"What's he going to do about Valentine?"

Nixon shrugged again.

"Talk to him, let him know we know he's here, I guess. Fact is he talked with him already, just didn't know who he was at the time."

"Valentine is a cool one, Tom," Targett warned. "He won't say anything he doesn't want to say."

"So what do we do?"

"Listen closely to what he says," Targett advised, "and read between the lines."

Targett looked around the room. The place was half full, but not yet full enough for the girls to be working.

"There's another thing you could do," Targett said.

"What?"

"Valentine talked to me about the girls, said he spent some time with Lisa."

"Fred said Lisa was up there with him now."

"Good," Targett said. "Talk to Lisa."

"About what?"

"About Valentine, about anything he might have said to her. She might be able to tell you something that he let slip."

"Would he do that?"

"Even the most closemouthed men let something slip during sex, Tom."

Nixon stared at Targett and said, "Were you ever a lawman?"

"No."

"Would you want to be?"

"No."

"Why not? I think you'd be good at it—a helluva lot better at it than I am."

"Give yourself some time," Targett said. "As to why *I* wouldn't want the job, there are too many restrictions and not enough benefits."

"Benefits?" Nixon asked sarcastically. "There are benefits?"

"Look at you," Targett said, "they didn't even give you a badge."

Nixon touched his shirt where the badge would be if he had it.

"It's coming."

"So's Christmas."

Nixon looked at his watch, finished his beer and said, "I got to meet Tilghman."

"Just remember what I said about Valentine."

"I'll remember," Nixon said before heading for the door. "Thanks."

As Tom Nixon exited the saloon Fred the bartender went upstairs and knocked on Valentine's door.

"Come in!" Valentine called.

Fred opened the door, stepped inside, and stopped. Lisa was sitting in bed next to Valentine, naked. She didn't bother to cover herself when she saw it was Fred. He had seen most of the girls naked at one time or another, but he had never sampled any of their charms. That was for the customers.

It wasn't Lisa's nakedness that made him stop, though. It was the gun in Valentine's hand.

"The bartender, right?" Valentine said.

"That's right."

"What do you want?" Valentine did not put the gun down.

"Just wanted to tell you, the marshal and his deputy are on their way up here to talk to you."

"They are, huh? I already talked to the marshal earlier today."

"I know, but he didn't know what you were then."

"And he knows now?"

"Yep."

Valentine frowned.

"Who told him?"

"I didn't."

Valentine remembered talking with Targett earlier in the day.

"No, it wasn't you," Valentine said.

"The boss, he doesn't want you to run—"

Valentine's laugh cut the bartender off.

"Why would I run?" Valentine asked. With his free hand he squeezed Lisa's thigh so hard that she winced. When he took his hand away Fred could see the red outline he left behind. "I got everything I want right here. Free food, free whiskey, free women. Why would I run?"

"Right," Fred said. "I, uh, the boss don't want you to tell them—"

"I know what to tell them," Valentine said. Fred breathed easier as the gunman finally laid the pearl-handle aside, on the table next to the bed. "You delivered your message, bartender."

Valentine roughly pulled Lisa to him and put his mouth on one of her breasts. Fred could see from the look on Lisa's face that she was not enjoying it.

He wished he could help her.

Her eyes seemed to be pleading with him to help her.

He backed out of the room and closed the door.

Tilghman met Nixon in front of the Long Branch right on time. "Is he here?"

"Upstairs," Nixon said. "He's got a room, and he's got a girl with him."

"Well," Tilghman said, "I hate like heck to interrupt the man when he's busy. Let's go and see what he has to say for himself."

Whatever Valentine was going to have to say, Nixon wished he knew how to read between the lines.

It was hard enough for him to learn how to read, at all.

Twenty-One

When Tilghman and Nixon entered the Long Branch everyone noticed. More than one man wondered if Tilghman was going to make them all stand up for a gun inspection.

Nixon, standing behind Tilghman, knew when the marshal spotted Targett, because the man's shoulders tensed. Tilghman ignored Targett and went to the bar.

"Marshal—" Fred said.

"Just stay where you are, Fred," Tilghman said. "What room is Valentine's?"

"Second door, Marshal, on the right."

Tilghman nodded and led the way up the steps. When he and Nixon got to the door he stood to one side, his deputy on the other. Tilghman knocked.

"Who is it?"

"Marshal Tilghman!"

"Just a minute."

When the door opened a girl Nixon recognized as Lisa stood there, naked. From the expression on her face she was not very happy. Nixon felt Tilghman stiffen and knew that Valentine had made the girl open the door just to embarrass Tilghman. Apparently, during the short conversation they'd had earlier in the day, Valentine had managed to read Tilghman right.

"Excuse me, miss—" Tilghman started, but that was as far as he got.

"Come on in, Marshal," Valentine called from inside. "Let the man in, honey, and come back to bed."

Lisa stepped away from the door, walked to the bed and got in next to Valentine. The gunman draped one arm across her shoulders and absently toyed with the nipple of one breast.

Tilghman walked in with Nixon behind him. Nixon saw the gun on the table next to Valentine's bed.

Tilghman looked around, spotted the girl's clothes, picked them up, and threw them to her.

"Excuse me, please, miss."

She started to get up from the bed but Valentine's hand tightened on her breast. She winced and wiggled, trying to get away from the pain.

"Let her up, Valentine!" Tilghman shouted.

Valentine glared at Tilghman, but his hand released the girl. She got up, thanked Tilghman with her eyes, and ran from the room without bothering to get dressed first.

"What do you mean by coming in here shouting at me, Marshal?" Valentine demanded.

Nixon moved to the other side of the bed, near Valentine's gun, and knew that the man had seen him.

"I came up here to talk to you, Valentine, not play games and watch you at your perversions."

"At my what?"

"I want to know what you're doing in town?"

Valentine's eyes moved from Tilghman to Nixon and back to Tilghman.

"If he don't move away from my gun, Marshal—"

"If you touch that gun, Valentine, I'll kill you,'" Tilghman said.

Valentine gazed at Tilghman with interest.

"You think you could, Marshal?"

"I know I can."

The two men stared at each other for a few moments before Tilghman said, "Move away from the man's gun, Tom. I want him to have a clear field for it if he wants to go for it."

"Well, Marshal," Valentine said, "I always said I wanted to die in bed, but this ain't quite what I had in mind."

"Nobody has to die today, Valentine," Tilghman said. "We just came here to talk."

Valentine folded his arms carefully over his chest and said, "So talk."

"What are you doing here?"

"Eating, drinking, whoring around. Practicing my—what did you call them—my perversions?"

"Your gun is for hire, Valentine," Tilghman said. "Who hired it this time?"

"I'm on vacation?"

"Why are you staying here rather than at the hotel?" Tilghman asked.

"Mr. Clark was kind enough to make this room available to me, free of charge."

"Why?"

Valentine frowned and said, "I think he's trying to show just how friendly a little town Dodge City can be."

"Then you don't work for Clark?"

"I can honestly say, Marshal," Valentine said, "that I have not done a lick of work for Mr. Clark."

"I see."

"Anything else, Marshal?"

"A few more questions, Mr. Valentine. How long do you intend to stay in town?"

"I don't rightly know, Marshal," Valentine said. "It does seem to be a friendly place."

"How friendly it stays depends entirely on you, Valentine."

"I'll remember that, Marshal," Valentine said, "I surely will."

"Tom," Tilghman said; directing Nixon to open the door.

Before leaving Tilghman said, "Valentine, I hope you don't intend to walk the streets of Dodge City with your gun on."

Valentine smiled. "That's a lie, Marshal."

"I beg your pardon?"

"I bet you hope I *do* walk the streets of Dodge with my gun on."

When Tilghman and Nixon got downstairs Clark was standing outside his office.

"I'll be right with you," Tilghman said to Nixon.

Nixon went on to the front of the saloon and waited there. Tilghman walked over to Clark.

"I have some advice for you, Clark."

"Oh, yeah? What is it?"

"Keep your hired killer right where he is," Tilghman said, "and don't give him anything more strenuous to do than change girls."

"What are you—"

"I know," Tilghman interrupted, "you don't know what I'm talking about."

"I don't."

"You can't think I'm that stupid, Clark," Tilghman said. "If you do, I feel sorry for you."

He turned and walked toward Nixon, and heard the office door close behind him. Every eye in the place was on him, and Tilghman saw that Targett was still sitting at the back table.

In the short time it took him to cross the room he remembered what Nixon had told him earlier, and what Flora had been telling him for a lot longer—he was a stubborn man and he knew that sometimes he let that stubbornness affect his judgment.

Maybe he was making that same mistake now, with Targett.

When he reached Nixon he said, "Go on back to your room and get some rest, Tom."

"What are you gonna do?"

"I'm going to talk to Targett," Tilghman said.

"About what?"

"Maybe you and Flora are right, Tom."

"Flora? What's she got to do with this?"

"Nothing," Tilghman said, "nothing at all."

Twenty-Two

Tilghman walked back across the room until he reached Targett's table. Targett looked up at him and waited for him to speak.

"Mind if I sit?" Tilghman asked.

"Go ahead," Targett said, "you're the law here, aren't you?"

"That doesn't mean you have to sit with me," Tilghman pointed out.

Targett considered that for a moment, then said, "Would you like to sit with me, Marshal?"

"Don't mind if I do," Tilghman replied. Targett had his back to the wall, so Tilghman sat to his right, leaving his gun hand free on the outside.

Once he sat down the rest of the patrons turned their attentions back to their own business.

"I . . . don't apologize easy," Tilghman started.

"It's not an easy habit to acquire," Targett said. "Besides, there's no need for it."

"Well, I think there is," Tilghman said, "so you'd better let me get it done."

Targett remained silent.

"I'm a little stubborn about the law," Tilghman said. "Maybe you noticed that."

Targett didn't answer.

"When I see somebody who bends it to their own means it rubs me the wrong way."

"I'd hate to see how you would have treated me if I had a reputation as a lawbreaker."

"But you don't," Tilghman said, "and my apology is for treating you as if you did. It wasn't fair of me, especially in light of the things you've done to help me."

"I wasn't helping you, exactly."

"You weren't? Why *did* you do what you did last night, then?"

Targett shrugged. "Just keeping the lid on."

"And what about telling Tom about Valentine?"

"I just wanted to tell Tom what to watch out for," Targett said. "I didn't want him making a wrong move."

"You like Tom, don't you?"

"As much as I like anyone, I guess."

"Well, he's taken a liking to you," Tilghman said, "and that should have been enough for me. See, I like Tom Nixon a lot, and I respect his opinion. I hope you and I can start over."

"Sure," Targett said.

"No grudge?"

"Well, I've held some grudges in my time," Targett said, "but I don't see anything worth holding one for here."

"That's good, Targett," Tilghman said. "I'd like to ask you a couple of questions now, if you don't mind."

"If it's about Valentine I told Tom everything I know about him."

"You never went against him?"

"No," Targett aid, "we were in the same place at the same time, but doing different jobs. We met, but that was about it."

"I see," Tilghman said. "Well, let me make you a proposition now."

"Go ahead."

"How would you like to be a deputy for a while?"

"How long is a while?"

"Just until this new law settles in. Dodge is a little big for Tom and me to split it in half."

"Wear a badge, huh?"

"As soon as we have them made up," Tilghman said.

Targett thought on it a moment, then decided he couldn't do it. He'd never worn a badge before, and he didn't want to start now.

"I've had a lot of jobs, Marshal," he said, "but I've always managed to avoid wearing a badge. If it's all the same with you, I'd just as soon keep it that way."

Targett saw Tilghman's jaw tighten.

"What's wrong with wearing a badge?"

"Now, don't take offense, Marshal," Targett said, "it's a find job, but it's for a man like you, not for a man like me."

"What kind of man is that?" Tilghman asked, and Targett could see that they were on the verge of getting off on that same wrong foot again—a second time."

"A man of high moral fiber, Marshal," Targett said. "That's you, not me. You're worthy of a badge like that, I'm not."

"You know something?" Tilghman said.

"What?"

"I don't believe you're shining me on," Tilghman said, "I think you really believe that."

"I do."

"All right, then," the lawman said, "I can accept your reasons. How's your horse doing?"

"Coming along. Another day or two."

Tilghman stood up and said, "At least I know that if you're not with me, you're not going against me."

"No, sir," Targett aid. "I wouldn't do that."

"No," Tilghman said, "I know you wouldn't. Thanks for talking to me, Targett."

"Thanks for changing your opinion."

"I didn't change my opinion," Tilghman said, "you did."

"Well, thanks just the same."

When Tilghman stepped outside he found Tom Nixon waiting for him.

"What are you doing here?"

"Waiting."

"For what?"

"You."

"I thought I told you to get some rest."

"I will."

"Well, what are you waiting for?"

"Nothing," Nixon said, "nothing at all."

Nixon turned to leave and Tilghman said, "Tom?"

"Yeah, Bill?"

"Come to the house for dinner later?"

Nixon smiled and said, "Sure, Bill. Tell Flora I'll be glad to come."

"Seven o'clock."

"I'll be there." Nixon turned and walked away.

Tilghman watched his friend go. He'd apologized to Targett and he owed an apology to Nixon, too, but he'd do that one special.

Over one of Flora's fine dinners.

Twenty-Three

"You looked pretty chummy with the marshal."

Targett looked up at Dan Clark, who was looking down at him expectantly.

"We made our peace," Targett said.

Clark looked behind him and waved, and Fred came over with another beer for Targett. Clark sat down.

"On the house," Clark said.

"Thanks," Targett said, but he didn't touch it.

"I've got a proposition for you, Targett."

"It's my day for propositions."

"Tilghman made you one?"

"Yes."

"About what?"

"He wanted me to wear a badge."

"And what did you say?"

"I said no."

"Why?"

"I'm not the type of man who would wear a badge."

"I could have told him that."

"You think so, huh?"

"I'm gonna make you a better offer than he did."

"I'm listening."

"Money, and a lot of it."

"To do what?"

"Work for me."

"Doing what?"

"Doing what I tell you."

"I never walk into a job blind, Clark," Targett said. "What would you be likely to tell me to do?"

"Well," Clark said, "I won't candy-coat it. Tilghman's new gun law will be the ruin of Dodge City. With him gone, the new law will go, too."

"You want me to kill Tilghman?"

"I might."

"Why?" Targett said. "You've got your hired killer with his pearl handle. Why me?"

"You can get close to Tilghman."

"You sent for Valentine before the new gun law, Clark," Targett said. "What did you want him for?"

"That's none of your business, Targett. I'm offering you a lot of money. Are you with me?"

"No."

"What?"

"I'd no more work for you than I would wear a badge," Targett said. "I'm not clean enough to wear a badge, but I sure as hell ain't dirty enough to work for you."

Clark sat back as if he'd been slapped. "Dirty, am I?"

Targett stared at the man, and realized Clark was honestly offended by what he had said. "Take it easy, Clark," he said.

"I'll show you who's dirty," the saloon owner said, standing up. "I don't want you in my place any more, Targett. Go drink somewhere else."

"But this is my favorite place, Clark," Targett said innocently. "You've got the best booze, the best bartender, the best women—"

"And they're all off limits to you," Clark said. "Maybe Tilghman will let you ride the fence, but if you're not *for* me, you're against me."

"If that's the way you want it," Targett said, standing up, "but I'll tell you one thing."

"What?"

Targett put his hat on and said, "If you send Valentine against me, you're going to be looking for a new killer."

Clark laughed.

"You ain't even carrying a gun."

"Haven't you heard?" Targett said. "It's against the law."

"That won't stop Valentine."

Targett took two steps towards the door and stopped.

"No, you're right," he said, "it won't. You know, you might have just given me the only reason in the world for wearing a badge."

After Target left, Clark went upstairs to Valentine's room.

"Who is it?"

"It's me," Clark shouted, and opened the door. He went in and stopped short when he saw Valentine's gun pointed at him.

"Can't be too careful," Valentine said, laying his gun aside. He was lying on the bed, fully dressed.

"I think it's time to put you to work, Valentine," Clark said.

"It's about time," Valentine said, swinging his feet to the floor. "Even free women and booze can get boring."

He stood up and strapped on his gun.

"Who's it gonna be, the deputy or the marshal?"

"Neither one just yet."

Valentine frowned and said, "Then who?"

"Fella named Targett."

"Targett?"

"You know him?"

"We've met, yeah."

"Well he's the joker in this deck, and I want him out of the way."

"What's his interest in all of this?"

"I don't know," Clark said, "but he's playing on Tilghman's side, might even be picking up a badge so he can carry a gun."

"Targett, wearing a badge?" Valentine scoffed. "He'd no more wear a badge than I would—unless you forced him into it."

"I didn't—"

"What did you say to him?"

"We had some words—"

"And you threatened him with me, huh?"

"I may have said—"

"Clark, let me tell you something," Valentine said. "When you are intending to kill a man you never tell him." He was speaking to Clark as a headmaster would speak to a student. "By telling him, you see, you either give him time to prepare to die, or to live—and if the man is a pro, like Targett, then you're really playing with fire."

"Are you telling me that you won't do this job?" Clark asked.

Valentine walked to the window in the room and looked out before answering.

"If by that you're asking me if I won't kill Targett," Valentine said, "no, I'm not telling you that, Clark. What I am telling you is that you've made my job harder, therefore it becomes more expensive. Can you understand that?"

Clark didn't like being spoken to as if he were a slow-learning child.

"Just do it," Clark said. "You'll get paid plenty, more than we agreed on. Just get it done."

"I'd like a little something in good faith, Mr. Clark," Valentine said.

Now Clark did a slow burn. "Come down to the office when you're ready and we'll take care of that," he finally replied.

"Fine," Valentine said, "just so long as we understand each other."

"Oh, we understand each other, Valentine," Clark assured him.

Clark glared at Valentine for a moment, then turned and left the room. Valentine smiled, knowing that he had insulted Clark. He was willing to bet that Targett had also insulted the man, because Targett would react to this *ass* the same way he did.

When Valentine was done with his job, he wondered who Clark would pay to try and kill *him*.

Twenty-Four

After dark.

Nixon had dinner with the Tilghmans, and after dinner Flora Tilghman had shooed them out of the kitchen so she could clean up. In the living room, over cigars and a brandy for Nixon, Tilghman had made his apologies and Nixon had accepted them.

Tilghman told Nixon about his conversation with Targett, and about Targett turning down his offer to wear a deputy's badge.

"There you go again, Bill," Nixon said. "You can't go using your own money to pay deputies."

"I know," Tilghman said, working some ash off the end of his cigar.

"I'm sure that if we need Targett he'll help us," Nixon said.

"That's just it," Tilghman said. "If we need him he can't help us, unless I give him a gun, and if I give him a gun and he's *not* a deputy, then I'm breaking the law myself. I hope you see why I can't do that?"

"I see it, Bill," Nixon said, "I don't understand it, but I see it."

"Targett said that badges were for men like me, who revered the law. He didn't say it that way, but that's what he meant."

"Well, that leaves me out then, Bill. I don't mind upholding the

119

law, but I don't revere it and I do question it, at times."

"I know you do," Tilghman said. "There's nothing wrong with questioning the law, I guess." However, his tone plainly said that there *was* something wrong with it.

"Bill, this new law . . ."

"Yes?"

"Do you really think it's going to work?"

"It's got to work, Tom," Tilghman said. "I see a time in the future when no one but law enforcement officials will carry guns—and that will be all over the country. And maybe there will be a time when we can do away with guns altogether—maybe all over the world!"

"I don't think either one of us will ever live to see that, Bill."

"I don't either, Tom," Tilghman said, "but maybe it will happen. Maybe."

Later that night Valentine slipped out of the Long Branch's back door, his gun strapped to his hip. He didn't know much about the way Dodge was set up, and he wanted to familiarize himself with the town's layout. He couldn't do it in the daytime because he wasn't about to go outside without his gun, and he wasn't quite ready to brace Tilghman or his deputy, yet.

He used the cover of darkness to scout out the town so that he'd be familiar with its setup when the time came for him to make his move.

He was playing in another man's game, and he had to make sure he knew the boundaries.

Rules were another matter. That was for the other man to worry about.

When Valentine played, there were no rules.

As he sat at his office desk Clark could hear the activities in the Long Branch starting to wind down, and it was only one A.M.

Clark wanted to open Dodge City up again, the way it used to be. First Bat Masterson had come along and done what he could to ruin Dodge. When Masterson left Clark felt he had a good chance to undo what Masterson had done, but then Tilghman became more prominent, even before they made him city marshal.

Clark had to rid Dodge of Tilghman so Dodge could revert to the goldmine it had once been for men like Dan Clark.

First, though, he had to make sure Targett was taken care of. After Targett was gone, then Valentine could concentrate on Tilghman.

And after Valentine took care of Tilghman, Clark was going to hire someone to take care of Valentine. Men like Targett and Valentine had to be taught their place. They could not be allowed to talk to Dan Clark the way they had today.

The Dan Clarks of the world were the leaders, and the sooner the Bill Tilghmans, and the Targetts, and the Valentines learned to accept that the better off everyone would be.

Even later that night Targett lay in his bed, alone. He'd had to resist taking Tanya back to his room again. For one thing, he didn't want her getting used to it, and for another he wanted to be able to lie alone and think.

He had several options. Up to now he had been largely a spectator to what was going on in Dodge. Okay, he had taken a *small* hand in things once or twice, but that was all. Now he was being put in a different position: if he stayed he might have to take a much more active role.

There had always been the chance he might have to go up against Valentine, and it was even more probable now that he had declared himself to Clark. For that he'd need a gun—but he wouldn't be able to carry a gun unless he took Tilghman's offer of a badge.

On the other hand he could just leave town, but he had really committed *himself* to staying and seeing what the outcome to all of this would be.

He got out of bed and walked over to the window. For a moment he thought he saw something beneath his window, a flash of light, perhaps a reflection of moonlight off something shiny.

Like nickel plate?

If he were Valentine he'd make sure he knew the lay of the town, and if Valentine were going to do that he'd have to do it at night, because Targett knew this was one man who'd never step one foot out onto the streets of Dodge City without his gun on his hip.

Targett went back to bed and put his gun on the night table, where he could get at it quickly.

Tomorrow morning he'd have to go and see Tilghman.

Valentine thought he had seen Targett standing at his window, but he couldn't be sure. He hoped that he had, and he hoped that Targett had seen him, as well.

It would give the big man something to think about.

Ever since Valentine and Targett had met in St. Louis, Valentine had wondered about him. Four years ago he had even checked Targett out, and he'd been impressed by what he had heard. From everything he'd learned he figured that Targett was the lawful version of himself. That is, where the law was an *invisible* line to Valentine, it was a very *visible* line to Targett, one that he was very careful never to cross completely.

Valentine felt that he and Targett were alike, but Targett fooled himself into thinking they weren't.

He didn't like it that his job suddenly was to kill Targett, but it *was* his job, and he'd do it.

Under other circumstances, he thought that he and Targett might even have become friends.

That would have been nice, because Valentine didn't have any friends.

Ah well, he wouldn't have known what to do with one, anyway.

Tilghman was walking Front Street, making the last of his rounds before he gave way to Tom Nixon. He was thinking about Targett, wondering what went through the mind of a man like that, when he thought he saw some movement over near the Dodge House.

He crossed the street to investigate, but when he got there the street and the walk in front of the hotel were empty, and so was the alley next to it. He went down the alley to check further. It was deserted, and there was no one behind the hotel.

He looked up and saw that all the windows were dark.

He wondered which window was Targett's.

Twenty-Five

Targett woke the next morning and remembered that Tilghman's shift was in the afternoon—if he and Nixon were sticking to their shifts. He'd have to wait until afternoon to talk to the marshal and make his counterproposal.

He went downstairs, had breakfast alone, and read the newspaper. There was a story on the arrests made the first day the new law was in effect, and how this indicated that Marshal Bill Tilghman was serious about enforcing it.

The talk that Targett heard in the dining room was about how unnecessary all of the arrests the previous day were, and how Tilghman was obviously getting carried away with his new job, overstepping his bounds.

Suddenly the man everybody liked and respected was the man everybody disliked and was eager to get rid of. See what happened when you put on a badge, Targett mused.

"It's not working, Bill," Mayor Wright said.

"What?" Tilghman wasn't sure he was hearing right.

"The new law, it's not working," Wright said. "I've been getting a lot of complaints about you."

"How many complaints?"

"A couple dozen."

"We made eight arrests," Tilghman said. "Where did the other sixteen complaints come from?"

"I don't—"

"I'll tell you where they came from," Tilghman said. "People who were put up to it by Dan Clark."

"Why Clark?"

"Clark wants this new law pulled more than anyone," Tilghman explained. "Also, if I say white he'll say black. That's the kind of relationship we have—if you can call it that."

"An adversary relationship?"

"That's a good way to put it."

"And he's using this new law to try and make you look bad?"

"That's right."

"I don't know, Bill," Wright said. "Mr. Clark is an important man in Dodge."

"He supported you for mayor, didn't he?"

"Well—"

"Did he *tell* you to recall this law?"

"What? Tell me?"

"He did, didn't he? He put pressure on you and you're folding."

"I'm doing no such thing," Wright said. "I'm reacting to complaints from the residents of this town—"

"Mayor, you can't cancel the new law after only one day," Tilghman said. "You haven't even given it a chance to work."

"Bill—"

"I'm telling you this law is going to be very important to Dodge, to the whole country—and to you . . . politically."

The word *politically* got to Wright.

"Well," he said, "we can let it go on a little longer, but if the council starts putting pressure on me—"

"Thank you, Mayor," Tilghman cut him off. "You'll see, in a matter of months, maybe weeks, you'll see the difference in this town."

"Weeks?" Wright said as Tilghman headed for the door. "Months? I didn't say anything about—"

Tilghman left the mayor's office and closed the door firmly behind him. He then went upstairs to his own office and found Targett sitting at his desk.

"What are you doing here?"

Targett looked around and said, "It's the only chair in the room."

Tilghman motioned Targett to get up, and he did. The marshal sat behind his desk and took a deep breath.

"I just came from the mayor's office," he said. "Mayor Wright wants to cancel the new law already."

"Why?"

"He's getting a lot of complaints, he says. That's because most of the people complaining are being put up to it by Dan Clark."

"Did you tell him that?"

"Yeah, but Clark supported him when he ran for mayor. Somehow I've got to prove that Clark is behind the complaints." Tilghman looked directly at Targett and said, "Was there something you wanted?"

"Yes," Targett said, "remember the proposition you made to me yesterday?"

"You've changed your mind?"

"Not exactly," Targett said. "I have a counterproposition for you."

"Well, let's hear it."

"You can swear me in as a deputy so I'll be able to carry a gun," Targett said, "but I don't want to wear a badge."

"Well, that wouldn't be too difficult," Tilghman said, "since we don't even have any deputy marshal badges yet . . ."

"Good."

"But I have reservations."

"I figured you would."

"You only want peace officer status so you can wear a gun, right?"

"That's right."

"Why?"

Targett told Tilghman about his conversation with Clark the day before, in the Long Branch.

"And you think Clark's going to send Valentine after you?"

"Somebody was outside my window last night," Targett said.

"And you think it was Valentine?"

"It makes sense," Targett said. "Before he makes a move he'd have to familiarize himself with the town, and he'd have to do that at night because he'd never go out on the street during the day without his gun."

"You know something," Tilghman said thoughtfully, "I thought I saw someone around the hotel last night, but it was only a fleeting shadow."

"That's all I saw, too," Targett said, "that and a glint of moonlight off something shiny."

"Like nickel plate?"

"Exactly."

Tilghman rubbed his jaw, looked up at Targett, and said, "Raise your right hand."

Targett obeyed, repeated after Tilghman, and swore to uphold the law of Ford County.

"Of course you realize your salary will be a little slow in coming," Tilghman said.

"You mean you get paid for this job?"

"*I* do, yes," Tilghman said.

"There's a message there," Targett said, "but we'll skip it for now."

"Now that you're a deputy," Tilghman said, "uh, do you intend to make rounds like the rest of us?"

"I think I'd like to be on the street during the day, Marshal," Targett said. "I want to be easy to find for Valentine."

"All right," Tilghman said. "I'll hang onto the three P.M. to three A.M. shift. You can work your shift out with Tom."

"Fine, and you'll let it be known that I *am* a deputy?"

"I'll inform the mayor now, and the newspaper."

"I'll go to the hotel and get my gun."

"Why don't you make some rounds with Tom and then he can introduce you as the new deputy. That way no one goes running to the mayor claiming that you're carrying a gun without being arrested."

"All right, Marshal, anything you say."

"And Targett?"

"Yeah?"

"Since we're going to be working together you might as well call me Bill."

"Sure, Bill," Targett said, "and you can call me Targett."

Twenty-Six

One of the people most surprised at the deputizing of Targett was Tom Nixon.

When Targett found him and informed him of the fact, Nixon believed him immediately because he didn't feel that Targett would kid about a thing like that.

"This is going to shock some people," Nixon said. "I know it shocks me."

"It's kind of a shock to me, too, Tom," Targett said, "but if Valentine is going to come looking for me, I want to be armed and ready."

"I can't say that I blame you for that," Nixon said. "Did you, uh, tell Bill exactly *why* you wanted to be deputized?"

"I did."

"How did he take it?"

"Considering everything that's been going on he took it surprisingly well," Targett said. "I think maybe he doesn't want my death on his conscience."

"Well, let's make some rounds and get it clear in people's minds that you *are* a deputy marshal," Nixon said. "The last thing in the world we need now are more complaints."

"Let's start with the sheriff," Targett suggested. "I don't want to run afoul of him."

"Good thought."

"And after the sheriff . . . let's go over to the Long Branch," Targett said slowly.

"Dan Clark told you he didn't want you in there anymore."

"I know," Targett said, "but that was before I became a deputy. Now I've got every right to enter the Long Branch anytime I want."

"And you want to rub his face in it?"

Targett smiled and said, "You betcha."

Bill Tilghman walked to his window and looked down at Tom Nixon in the street.

He hoped he hadn't made a mistake by swearing Targett in as a deputy. Only time would tell—and it wouldn't take that long, either.

Now it was time to go down and inform the mayor.

Twenty-Seven

Sheriff Sughrue was obviously surprised by the news.

"It was my understanding that Marshal Tilghman wanted you out of town as soon as possible."

Targett smiled and said, "We made up."

Sughrue looked at Nixon, who shrugged and said, "They made up."

Sughrue looked at Targett and asked, "What's really behind this?"

Targett looked at Nixon, who nodded.

"There's a hired killer in town named Valentine."

"Valentine?" Sughrue said, frowning. "I've never heard of him."

"I don't think he usually works this far west," Targett said. "Anyway, we have reason to believe that he's working for Dan Clark."

"And Clark is going to send him after Tilghman?" Sughrue asked.

"Me first," Targett pointed out, "and then Tilghman."

"Ah-hah," Sughrue said, "so you needed to carry a gun and Tilghman cooperated."

"Right."

"Well," Sughrue said, shrugging, "if Tilghman can cooperate and he doesn't even like you, I guess I can go along."

Targett stared at Sughrue for a few moments until the sheriff finally said, "Oh, I don't have any feelings about you one way or the other."

Targett nodded and said, "Me, too."

When Targett and Nixon entered the Long Branch, Fred's eyes widened.

"Hey, Targett," the barkeep said, as they approached the bar, "I'm supposed to call the boss if you ever come in here again."

"So go tell him," Targett said, "but first give us two beers."

"Jeez," Fred said, setting the beers down in front of them nervously, "we got bouncers here, ya know. The boss will have them throw you out on your rear, and none too gentle, either."

"Go and tell him I'm here, Fred," Targett responded, "and then stand back and watch."

Fred looked from one to the other a couple of times and then said, "Okay, it's your funeral."

Fred came out from behind the bar and went to the office. They watched as he knocked, entered, and came out in a few seconds.

"He's livid," Fred said in a hoarse whisper. "I'm supposed to signal the bouncers."

"Signal them."

Fred swallowed hard and then raised his arm and waved his hand. Just as two men got up from a table and approached Targett, Clark came out of his office to watch.

As the two bouncers reached Targett he drew his gun and pointed it at them. Both men nervously looked back at Clark to see what they should do.

"They want you to tell them if they should live or die, Clark," Targett said.

"Hey, hey!" Clark shouted. He approached the bar, pointing at Targett. "He's got a gun. That's against the law. You're a deputy, Nixon, arrest him."

Some of the patrons in the Long Branch started shouting the same thing.

"So's he," Tom Nixon said.

"What?" Clark said, stopping short.

"I said he's a deputy, too," Tom Nixon repeated.

Clark stared at them for a few moments, leaving his two bouncers hanging.

"I don't believe it," Clark finally sputtered.

"Call off your dogs," Targett said.

The thought of calling off his men obviously rankled Clark, but in the face of this new information he had no choice.

"Back away," he said, tightly.

The two men backed up and returned to their table. Targett holstered his gun and then looked at Clark.

"I don't believe this," the Long Branch owner said.

Targett picked up his beer and said, "You said that already."

"How did this happen?" Clark asked Tom Nixon. "This man is not even a resident of Dodge City. He's a stranger in town!"

"There's another stranger in town, too, Mr. Clark," Nixon said, "named Valentine. The marshal just thought we might need an extra gun on the street."

Clark moved closer to Targett and said, "You think this is going to put you out of my reach?"

Targett raised his eyebrows and said, "That sounds like a threat to me."

Targett looked at Tom Nixon and Nixon said, "Sounded like a threat to me, too."

"And against an officer of the law, too."

"And Fred's a witness," Nixon said.

Fred looked frightened, all of a sudden.

"Fred works for me," Clark said. "He's not a witness to anything I don't *tell* him he's a witness to."

Targett looked at Nixon and said, "I've got to stop drinking. That almost made sense to me."

"Look," Clark growled, "I want you out of my place . . . now!"

"Maybe you didn't understand, Mr. Clark," Targett said. "I'm a peace officer. I have a right to go anywhere I want. I do have my rounds to make, you know."

"Make them somewhere else," Clark said, forcefully. "I don't want you here!"

Targett looked at the beer that remained in his mug. It was half empty—or half full, depending on how much of an optimist you were.

He threw the rest of it in Clark's face, and then grabbed the man by his shirt, bunching it up in his hands. He pulled up, lifting Clark up onto his toes, putting him in a totally defenseless position. Without his heels on the floor Clark had no balance and could make no countermove.

"Targett . . ." Nixon said, warningly, but Targett knew exactly what he was doing.

He was humiliating Dan Clark in front of a room full of witnesses.

"Now listen to me, Clark," Targett said, "if I had a badge right now I'd pin it to your ass, but I don't have one yet. When I do, I'll be back to do just that. Do you understand me?"

He released Clark and pushed him . . . hard. Clark staggered back, his legs pedaling beneath him, trying to catch his balance. He might have, too, if he hadn't stepped into a spittoon. His foot slid right out from under him and he fell on his back.

Everyone in the place forgot who it was on the floor and started to laugh. Clark pushed himself to a seated position and glared at Targett, and then around at everyone else.

The laughter in the place was so loud Targett almost missed what Clark had to say.

"You just made a very bad mistake," the saloon owner said. "Your last."

"Don't make me laugh, Clark," Targett said, leaning over so

Clark would be sure to hear him, "but then again, you already have."

Targett laughed forcefully, then turned and walked out of the saloon with Tom Nixon.

"Do you know what you just did?" Nixon said outside. "You made him a laughingstock in his own place. He ain't gonna forget that."

"I know what I did," Targett said. "I just made sure he'd send Valentine after me."

"If I were you," Nixon said, "I wouldn't be so happy about that."

Twenty-Eight

Inside the saloon Dan Clark got to his feet and glared at each of the laughing patrons of the Long Branch. Behind the bar Fred was *not* laughing, because he knew if he did he would have to pay for it.

Clark continued to stare at the men in the saloon and little by little the laughter began to trail off. Eventually, it became deadly silent in the saloon, and Clark turned and walked back to his office. He went inside, picked up a chair, and threw it against the wall. Then he took off his jacket and threw that, then proceeded to brush sawdust and dirt off his pants.

He went out his office's back door and took the back stairs to the second floor. He thought about going to his room first to change but decided to go and see Valentine while his anger was still white-hot.

He entered the gunman's room without knocking. Valentine leapt off the woman he was with. Clark didn't even recognize the naked woman as Jean, one of his saloon girls. He just shouted, "Get out!"

Jean jumped off the bed, seizing the opportunity to get away from Valentine, and ran to the door, her sizable breasts bobbing and bouncing.

Valentine lay with his back on the bed, his gun in his hand.

"What the hell—" he said.

"I want it done today!" Clark ordered.

Valentine noticed Clark's disheveled appearance then and asked, "What happened to you?"

"Targett put his hands on me," Clark said tightly, adding angrily, "and humiliated me in my own place. I want him dead, Valentine, and I want him to know who sent you before you kill him. I want him to know *why* he is dying, and who he has to thank for it."

Valentine studied Clark for a few moments and said, "I can't do it that way."

"What?" Clark exploded. "Why not?"

"I told you before, Targett is a professional," Valentine replied, laying his gun aside and sitting up. "I can't afford to play a game with him like that. If I'm gonna kill him I'm just gonna have to kill him."

"Can't afford?" Clark said. "You can't *afford* to? I'll tell you what you can afford and what you can't afford, Valentine."

"Now listen, Clark—"

"No, you listen!" Clark shouted. "Ten thousand dollars!"

There was a moment of stunned silence.

"What?" Valentine asked.

"I will pay you ten thousand dollars to kill Targett just the way I said," Clark stated.

Valentine licked his lips.

"Ten thousand dollars?"

Clark grinned in triumph. "Now can you *afford* to do it?"

Valentine rubbed his jaw with his right hand, thinking about what he could do with ten thousand dollars.

"I want half of it up front."

"Done!" Clark said. "Give me a chance to clean up and come to my office in an hour."

"You know why Targett did what he did, don't you?"

"Yes," Clark said, "because he is tired of living."

"Listen to me carefully, Clark," Valentine said. "He did it to force you into sending me after him. He'll know I'm coming, which will make it that much harder."

"For ten thousand dollars," Clark said, "you'll find a way—"

"I'm not complaining about the money," Valentine cut him off, "but I'm going to need some backup."

"You name it and I'll get it for you."

Valentine thought a moment.

"Four men," Valentine said, "and they have to be able to use a gun. I don't want some shit-kicker who will shoot himself in the foot."

"You'll have your four men," Clark said, "and don't worry, they'll be able to shoot."

"All right, then," Valentine said. "I'll see you in an hour."

Clark nodded, left the room, and went back to his own. He slammed the door behind him and rubbed his hands together with excitement. He removed his pants and threw them into a corner to be discarded.

Tonight Targett would be dead.

Tonight was a night that Clark would need one of the women. He knew Tanya had been with Targett a few times. *He* would have Tanya tonight, while Targett was being killed.

That would be poetic justice.

As angry as Clark was, it never once dawned on him to pull the trigger on Targett himself.

Valentine got out of bed and got dressed. He had not finished with the woman—not by a longshot—and he was still hard and erect-but now it had nothing to do with the woman.

Ten-thousand dollars!

He had never had that much money at one time in his life. He'd be able to go anywhere he wanted, maybe to New Orleans, where he could try some of them Cajun women, or even to San Francisco, for some of those Chinese whores.

That would be fitting, wouldn't it? After killing Targett and being paid ten thousand dollars, to go to Targett's home city and spend the money?

Valentine picked up his gunbelt and put it on. He had never bushwhacked a man before. He'd killed a lot of men—he'd lost count, by now—but they had all been facing him and not one of them had had a gun at his back.

He had never even *thought* about bushwhacking a man before, but for ten thousand dollars he would bushwhack his own mother.

He hoped that Clark would supply him with four competent men. The chances were he was going to have to deal with Targett and at least one of the lawmen, either the marshal or the deputy. He was going to have to make that clear to Clark, as well, but he didn't think Clark would object. Jesus, the man was so mad now he had forgotten his priorities. When he'd first contacted Valentine the most important thing in the world to him was to rid Dodge City of Bill Tilghman.

Now all he could think of was getting revenge on Targett.

Dan Clark was, at best, a dangerously unstable man, and once Valentine got his ten thousand dollars he was going to hightail it as far from Dodge City as possible.

Twenty-Nine

Targett and Nixon found Tilghman in the office and told him what had happened at the Long Branch. Tilghman listened intently, but both Targett and Nixon could tell from the look on his face that he was not happy about what had occurred.

When they finished the story Tilghman was silent for a few moments. "I don't know that I approve of this," he said, finally.

"I knew you wouldn't," Targett said.

"And you did it anyway?" Tilghman asked. "Was this your plan when you agreed to be deputized?"

"No," Targett said, "grabbing Clark was a spur of the moment idea. I only wanted to let him know I was deputized, and that I was carrying a gun."

"Why did you do this, then?"

"See if you can understand this, Bill," Targett said patiently, "I didn't want to have to wait around for Valentine to come for me. I didn't want to feel like I was walking around Dodge with a target painted on me. This way I forced both Clark's hand, and Valentine's."

"When do you think he'll try for you?"

"Oh, tonight," Targett said, "it will have to be tonight. Clark was

143

too angry for it to be any other way. He'll order Valentine to do it tonight, and will probably promise him a bonus."

"Will he come alone?" Nixon asked.

"No," Targett replied.

"Does he have a reputation for bushwhacking?" Tilghman asked.

"No, all of Valentine's previous work that I know of has been face-to-face."

"Work?" Tilghman said, his tone heavy with irony. "Is that what you call it?"

"Why wouldn't he come alone tonight?" Nixon wanted to know.

"Clark will want me to know why I'm dying," Targett said. "He's going to want Valentine to talk to me, first. To do that, Valentine's going to need some backup. He won't take a chance of playing that kind of game with me."

"Then you'll need backup, as well," Tilghman noted.

"I was hoping you'd see it that way," Targett said.

Valentine took the five thousand dollars Dan Clark paid him and stuck it in his pocket. There was just no place else to put it where it would be safe.

Clark had paid Valentine and then called in the four men he had chosen to work with the hired gun. Valentine didn't say a word to them until Dan Clark got up and left the room. Then he explained how he intended to kill Targett.

"What do we do if the marshal or his deputy come along?" one of the men asked.

"We'll have to take care of them, too."

The men backed off a bit at the thought of killing a lawman.

"I'm sure Mr. Clark will make it more than worth your while," Valentine said, and that appeased them some.

"All right, everyone out the back way," Valentine said. "Meet me at the north end of town at midnight."

"That's where the marshal lives."

"I know," Valentine said, "they won't expect us to meet there."

"Wait a minute," the man said. "Are they expecting us at all?"

"They're expecting me," Valentine said. "You fellas are gonna be a surprise."

The four men went out the back way and Valentine called Clark back into his own office.

Before Valentine left Clark's office he said, "Make sure you're in the Long Branch from midnight on."

"I'll be there," Clark replied. "I'll be listening for the shots."

"You might not hear them," Valentine said, "but I'll be back when the job's done, for the rest of my money."

"You'll get it," Clark said.

Yeah, Valentine said, I'll get it in the back if I'm not careful.

But Valentine was always careful. Valentine went out the back door. There were still a few hours before dark, and Clark wondered where Valentine would spend them.

He hoped that his men had understood the instructions *he* had given them before they had talked to Valentine.

Thirty

As midnight approached Targett was on the streets of Dodge City, ostensibly making his rounds. He hoped that the plan he had devised would work. The last time he had seen everyone, they had all claimed to know what their part was, but he was still putting his life in the hands of three men he had never worked with before. He went over the meeting he'd had earlier. . . .

Targett, Tom Nixon, Bill Tilghman, and Sheriff Pat Sughrue were all in the sheriff's office as darkness approached.

"Now, does everybody understand what they have to do?" Targett asked.

Tilghman and Nixon nodded, and Pat Sughrue said, "Yes, but are you sure this is going to work?"

"No, Sheriff, I'm not at all sure that it's going to work," Targett said, "but I'm betting that it will."

"Yeah," Tom Nixon said, "you're betting your life."

"I still think we should be closer," Tilghman persisted.

"If you're too close he won't make a move," Targett explained. "We've gone over this, Bill. It's the only way it can work."

"There's something I don't understand," Pat Sughrue said.

"Tell me what it is and I'll try to explain it to you," Targett said.

"Why are you doing this?" Sughrue asked. "I mean, why not just ride out and head back home?"

"That's a good question," Targett said.

"You got a good answer?" Nixon asked.

Targett thought a moment, then said, "No, I don't. Maybe afterward, I will."

"If there is an afterward," Tilghman said.

"Yeah . . . " Targett said.

It was midnight and Targett was on Front Street. Something was bothering him, now. He was as alert as he could possibly be, and he couldn't detect anyone else on the street. He *knew* that Tom Nixon was supposed to be across the street behind him, in the shadows, but he didn't like the fact that he couldn't detect him.

Nixon couldn't be that good.

Nixon knew he had messed up.

When the man came up behind him and stuck the gun in his ear, he knew that Targett had trusted him, and now he'd gone and gotten him killed for sure.

It never occurred to Nixon that he was as good as dead, too.

Valentine stood in the darkness, watching the deputy. Targett was stupid to think that Valentine wouldn't *know* that he'd have backup. The deputy was a full block behind Targett, keeping to the shadows, but the streets were so empty that he was able to always keep Targett in sight.

Valentine just stood still and waited for the deputy to draw abreast of him, and then stepped out behind the man and stuck his gun in his ear.

"Don't move, don't make a sound," Valentine whispered. He felt the deputy tense. "Relax, Deputy. You don't want to die, yet."

Later, Valentine said to himself, as he took the deputy's gun from his holster, but not yet.

Nixon's mind was racing over Valentine's words.

He *didn't* want to die, but if he forced Valentine to shoot, at least the shot would warn Targett.

He thought about it and thought about it, and then knew that he wouldn't do it.

He just wasn't that brave.

Tilghman did not see what had happened to Nixon. He was too busy watching Targett. He marveled at how utterly relaxed the man looked down on the street, even though he knew that death could come at him from the darkness at any moment.

Tilghman wondered if he would be as calm.

He certainly wasn't that calm *now.*

Valentine marched Nixon behind the buildings on Front Street until they reached the livery stable. He walked the deputy right up to the rear door.

"Open it," he ordered.

"I can't," Nixon said. "It's locked."

"Don't play games, Deputy," Valentine said. "You own the place. Now take out the key and open it."

Nixon obeyed, taking the key out of his pocket and unlocking the door. As he opened it Valentine pushed him and he tripped and sprawled onto the stable floor. Valentine came in behind him, and then Nixon became aware of more men following after Valentine.

"Find a lamp," he heard the killer instruct someone.

There was some moving around, then someone bumped into something and cursed aloud. Nixon hoped that whoever it was had broken his foot.

"Got one," someone said.

He heard a match strike and the glow illuminated the man who was holding it. The man lit the lamp he was holding and the interior of the stable became visible.

"All right," Valentine said to the man with the lamp, "keep him here, and keep him *quiet!*"

"Right."

Valentine turned to three other men and said, "Let's go."

As Valentine and the others left, the fourth man took out his gun and pointed it at Nixon. The lawman thought about the feed bin near the office. There was a handgun in there, wrapped in cloth. It had been there a long time, in case of emergency, and this was certainly an emergency.

The only thing he wasn't sure of was whether the gun would fire or not. He hadn't checked the weapon in a long time.

Even when you put something away for an emergency, who ever expects the emergency to happen? he mused.

He guessed he would find out the hard way if the gun worked.

Targett walked slowly, his eyes cutting through the darkness ahead of him, and on either side of him. He wondered idly if Valentine would sink to shooting him in the back from some rooftop or doorway.

Suddenly he got an itch right in the center of his back, where he couldn't reach it.

He hoped that Dan Clark had not bought Valentine's soul as well as his gun.

He was tense inside, but made every attempt to seem calm on the outside. He was still bothered by the fact that he couldn't detect any sign of Tom Nixon on his tail. Once he almost turned around and went back to check, but that wouldn't have been wise. If he was being watched by Valentine, it would have given Tom Nixon away—if he was there, at all.

He was *supposed* to be there!

Jesus, you better be there, Tom.

He wondered who he was more worried about, himself or Nixon?

Thirty-One

Targett guessed it was close to one o'clock.

The only noise he heard was the sounds of reverie coming from several saloons, including the Long Branch.

Targett stopped into some of the saloons, just to put in an appearance—including the Long Branch. His stop there drew him a dirty look from Dan Clark, who was sitting alone at a back table, and a worried look from Fred the bartender, who was probably afraid that Targett was going to ask for a drink.

Targett matched stares with Clark for a few seconds and then backed out of the saloon, feeling silly.

Outside he paused and looked up and down the street. He was now convinced that Tom Nixon was *not* behind him.

The only question in his mind now was whether or not the man was still alive.

Nixon was trying to get comfortable on the floor of the livery when the man with the gun said, "Don't move."

"I'm just getting comfortable," Nixon complained. "You don't look so comfortable, either."

"I ain't."

"See? Why don't we both move into the office where we can both be more comfortable?"

The man narrowed his eyes and said, "I don't know."

"I didn't hear Valentine say we couldn't move, did you?"

The man thought a moment and then answered, "No."

"All right, then," Nixon said. "Let's go. I might even have a bottle of whiskey in there."

The man didn't say anything, so Nixon gathered his legs beneath him and started to stand.

Valentine positioned three of his men and himself at the south end of Front Street. He put two of them on one side, and kept one with him on the other. After taking the deputy off of Front Street he had checked it again and saw no one else following Targett.

He had chosen the south end of town to kill Targett. The livery was nearby, along there were a few homes, but it was far enough down the street from the saloons and hotels that he shouldn't have to worry about anyone coming along by accident. The street actually narrowed some here, and was also darker than in other places.

It was a perfect spot.

Targett turned around when he hit the town's north end and started walking south. It must have been close to one-thirty. Was it possible that Valentine *wasn't* going to make his move tonight?

Anything was possible, but Targett couldn't believe that he had read Dan Clark *that* wrong. After what happened in the Long Branch, a man like Clark would want *instant* revenge. He wouldn't be willing to wait a day or two.

Targett was just going to have to keep walking back and forth, waiting for Valentine to make his move.

All this walking, making rounds.

He wondered if all lawmen had flat feet?

Sughrue, positioned at the north end of town on the roof of the Feed & Grain, heaved a sigh of relief when Targett turned and started south.

If he kept sighing every time Targett made that turn safely he was going to run out of breath, he thought.

At the south end of town Bill Tilghman was positioned on the roof of the home of one of Dodge's town council members, Del Lunden. Del and his family had been quietly moved to the hotel for the night. This was the darkest part of town, and anyone could hide in the shadows given off by nearby trees and shrubs. Tilghman squinted his eyes, trying to penetrate the darkness and see if he was right that there was someone on the other side of the street.

Could it be Nixon? No, he was supposed to be following *behind* Targett, and off the street, not positioning himself ahead of him.

Tilghman stared harder, wondering if he was imaging it or—wait! There it was. Movement, and a glint of something in the moonlight.

The nickel plating of a gun?

Nixon made it to his feet without getting shot and said, "The office is right over here, and there are two chairs inside. We can be comfortable while we wait."

"All right," the man with the gun said, finally. "Move."

Nixon led the way to the office, which was dark because the light from the lamp wasn't reaching that far.

"Wait," the man said, "it's too dark."

"You afraid of the dark?"

"No." The man's reply was quick—too quick. "It's just . . . too dark."

"There's a lamp inside," Nixon said. "Look, I'll light a match."

He struck the match against the wall and then held if aloft.

"See? Light? And there's the lamp, hanging on the wall."

He took the lamp off the office wall, lit it with the match, and put it down on the desk.

"See? Two chairs."

"Sit down."

"Sure," Nixon said, and started to sit.

"Not there," the man said, "get away from the desk."

"Okay, take it easy," Nixon said. He moved away from the desk and sat down.

"Where's the whiskey?"

"It should be in one of the drawers."

One by one the man opened the drawers to peer in. Nixon prayed that he would come up with an idea before the man got to the last drawer and realized that there was no whiskey.

As Targett approached the south end of town it felt different to him. The street narrowed here, and although not significantly so, it was still the ideal spot for an ambush.

He'd passed this way half a dozen times already, but now it felt different.

His senses told him something *was* different, something was wrong—or right, depending on how you looked at it.

Thirty-Two

"Stop right there, Targett!" Valentine said.

He admired Targett for his reaction. He didn't start or show any kind of surprise, he just did as he was told and stopped.

A pro.

Targett expected the voice just before he heard it, and was actually already in the act of stopping.

Now he just waited for what came next.

More instructions?

A shot?

"Stop right there, Targett!" Tilghman heard.

It was so quiet at this end of town that the voice drifted up to the roof Tilghman was on and could almost have been right next to him.

Tilghman picked up his rifle, leaned it on the edge of the roof, and waited.

"All right." Targett said after a few moments. "What now, Valentine? Want me to turn around so you can put one in my back?"

"I wouldn't do that, Targett."

"You brought help, didn't you?"

"Yes," Valentine said. "One here with me, two across the street."

Targett wished Valentine had been a little more specific about where the other men were.

"*I* didn't think *you'd* do that."

"You brought help, too," Valentine said, "only I took care of him already."

"Is he alive?"

"The deputy is alive . . . for now," Valentine said.

"And what about me?"

"You're alive, too . . . for now."

"For how long?"

"Until you know why you're dying."

"Come on out where I can see you, Valentine. Grant me that."

There was a moment of silence, and then Valentine stepped out of the shadows into the moonlight. Targett knew there were two men behind him, and one more ahead of him. He committed to memory the place from where Valentine had stepped forward. The other man was either just to the right, or left of that space

"Here I am, Targett."

Targett committed that to his just actions. He heard it, and was relat—

From his vantage point Tilghman could see the entire street. He watched Valentine step out into the moonlight and sighted the gunman down the barrel of his rifle—then decided he was wrong. Targett would take care of Valentine. Tilghman looked into the shadows. He had heard Valentine tell Targett that there were three other men in the shadows. He had also heard what the man said about Nixon, but he couldn't worry about his friend now. He sighted down the barrel into the darkness, hoping for a glimpse of something he could fire at.

Even if he did see something, though, he felt Targett was in an indefensible position. Even if Targett killed Valentine, and Tilghman killed one other man, there were still two men left to kill Targett. Tilghman wouldn't be able to locate them and kill them both before at least one of them got off a shot.

Targett was as good as dead.

* * *

The man with the gun closed the last desk drawer and looked at Nixon. There was a hurt look on his face.

"There's no whiskey here."

"There isn't?" Nixon said, contriving to look puzzled. "There should be."

"Well, there ain't," the man said. "You lied to me."

"I didn't lie," Nixon said. "Look, that old man I've got running the place must have drank all the whiskey."

The man continued to stare at Nixon, holding his gun in one hand and rubbing his mouth with the other. Looking for the whiskey had worked up a thirst in him.

"Wait a minute," Nixon exclaimed. "I remember now. I put a bottle away, so the old man wouldn't be able to find it."

"Where?"

"Let me think." Nixon purposely let the silence lengthen until the other man became impatient.

"Come on, come on—"

"I know!" Nixon said, standing up. He knew he was taking a chance with the sudden move, but the man didn't shoot him.

"Where?"

"Out here," Nixon said, pointing. "I left it out here in the feed bin. I'll get it."

"Wait! Hold it!"

Nixon didn't stop. His stomach muscles clenched as he waited for the man to shoot.

"It's right in here," he said, lifting the lid of the grain bin. He drove his hand in among the grain, groping for the gun.

"Get back!" the man ordered. "I'll find it!"

Nixon was close to panic. Where the hell was it?

"What do we do now?" Targett said.

"I'm supposed to tell you why you're dying."

"I know all that," Targett said, "I insulted Clark, I humiliated him—"

"Knowing he'd send me after you tonight."

"Yes."

"And you had the deputy back you up," Valentine said. "I'm surprised you didn't have more—"

Valentine stopped in midsentence. The gunman's eyes went up to the roof where Tilghman was. He was good, Targett thought. He had immediately figured from which roof a man would have the best view of the street. When the killer looked back at him he knew he was going to make his move.

Targett was not a gunman. He could hit what he aimed at, but he knew he'd never outdraw Valentine.

Even as he went for his gun, he knew he'd never make it.

"I said get away!" the man with the gun shouted.

Nixon tensed and waited for the bullet to come, and then his hand touched something.

"I've got it!" he cried out triumphantly.

It was no act. He could feel the gun beneath the cloth. He dug into the grain with his other hand, trying to free the gun from the cloth so he could come out of the grain bin firing.

"Well, come on," the man said, "bring it out."

Nixon's hand closed over the butt, and his finger slid into the trigger guard.

"Here it comes," he said.

He pulled the gun free of the grain and turned. The cloth was still on it, but he pulled the trigger and the bullet punched through the cloth and into the chest of the man.

Thirty-Three

At the sound of the shot Valentine took his eyes off Targett, even though they were both already drawing their guns.

Targett threw himself to the right, rolling on the ground. Valentine, even though he had looked away, still got his gun out first, but by the time he fired Targett was already on the ground moving.

"Get him!" Valentine shouted.

Tilghman heard the shot from the livery but knew that Targett's life depended, in part, on him. He continued to sight down the barrel and suddenly a man came out of the shadows, his gun pointed at Targett.

Still figuring that Valentine was Targett's, Tilghman pulled the trigger of his rifle and the man was thrown back into the shadows.

When Sughrue heard the first shot he started running for the roof hatch, trying to get down to the street level in time to help. He was halfway down when he heard the second shot, and then it sounded like all hell had broken loose.

He started running to the south end of town as fast as he could.

* * *

The cloth on the gun had caught fire and Nixon shook it off and then stamped it out. He heard the shot from outside. He relieved the dead man of his gun and tucked it into his belt on the way to the door.

Valentine saw Tilghman's muzzle flash from the roof and returned fire.

"Shoot, damn it!" he shouted at the men across the street.

The two men had been afraid to fire for fear of hitting Valentine. Now they fired at Targett, but never came close because Targett kept moving. He could hear lead striking the dirt around him. Eventually he'd have to stop rolling, and he knew Valentine—the pro that he was—would be waiting for that moment.

Valentine backed up, seeking the refuge of the darkness of a doorway. His eyes were on Targett now, who was just coming to a stop. Valentine thought he moved very fast for a big man.

But not fast enough.

Nixon raced from the livery and saw the muzzle flashes from across the street, but dared not fire for fear of hitting Targett.

He had to get closer to the action.

Tilghman saw Nixon running and breathed a sigh of relief that the man was alive. Valentine was in the dark and out of sight, but Tilghman fired several times into the dark to cover both Nixon and Targett.

Valentine ducked as the bullets chewed up the door of the building behind him, showering him with splinters and glass. Targett had come to a stop on one knee, looking for a target. Valentine fired at Targett and saw the bullet strike the big man high on the left shoulder.

Targett went down on his back and Valentine started counting his ten-thousand dollars.

Sughrue was running down Front Street, now filled with people who had come out of the saloons. When he reached the south end of town he saw Targett down on one knee, and then he heard a shot and saw Targett go down on his back.

Valentine saw Sughrue approaching, but Tilghman fired again from the roof, causing the killer to duck again.

Sughrue had seen the muzzle flash from the dark and he fired at it and ran to Targett.

"Get out of the way, damn it!" Targett snapped.

There were too damned many people on the street now, and things were starting to go wrong.

With Tilghman firing from the roof, and Nixon and Sughrue on the street, Targett felt he had too much help, now. A case in point was the fact that he had been about to fire at Valentine when Sughrue reached him and got in his way. Instead, Valentine fired, and the bullet struck Sughrue in the shoulder.

"Shit," Targett said, "I told you to get out of the way!"

Sughrue groaned and Targett grabbed him beneath the arms and started to drag him out of the street. Nixon saw this and fired where he thought Valentine was, to cover them.

Valentine also cursed the presence of Sughrue. If not for him his shot might have finished Targett. He still needed to put one more bullet in the man to finish the job.

Tilghman, seeing Targett dragging Sughrue, made a move to stand up on the roof so he could better cover them. Instead, he lost his footing on the slanted roof, fell on his butt, shouted, "Damn!" and slid down off it. He landed hard and although he wasn't seriously hurt, he lost hold on his rifle.

Valentine's other two men had frozen when the shooting started. Now they saw Nixon and Sughrue, and they heard Tilghman firing from the roof. They didn't actually know who the three men were, but that made three more than they had signed on for.

"Let's get out of here," one of them whispered.

"Good idea," the other said, and they took off.

Nixon saw the two men starting to run and pegged two shots at them. He thought he hit one, but they kept running down the street, staying to the shadows.

He had no way of knowing whether or not one of them was Valentine, so he kept on shooting.

Targett had dragged Sughrue to safety and shouted at Nixon, "Let them go. Valentine's over there, across the street."

Nixon obeyed and looked where Targett was pointing.

"How bad is it?" Targett asked.

"My arm," Sughrue said. "I think I'm all right, though."

"I think I am, too," Targett said.

He grabbed Sughrue's kerchief and pressed it against the man's wound, and then touched his hand to his own gunshot wound. He was bleeding pretty good. He used his own kerchief to try to stop the bleeding.

Nixon took up the position vacated by the other two men, directly across from Valentine.

Tilghman was still on the ground. He had found his rifle, but when he tried to stand, pain flashed through his right ankle.

He was not a man given to frequent use of profanity, but the circumstances were special.

"Double Damn!" he said.

"Where are we?" Sughrue asked Targett.

"We're on the same side of the street as Valentine," Targett said.

"The others?"

"Nixon's across the street, Tilghman was on the roof, but now I don't know. He hasn't fired a shot in a few minutes. Valentine is alone, as far as I can tell."

"Leave me here," Sughrue said. "We've got to block off the other side, near the livery. Go around."

"You'll be all right?"

"Yeah," Sughrue said. "Where's my gun?"

"Here," Targett said, handing it to him. He'd picked it up when he started dragging Sughrue from the street and tucked it into his belt.

"Okay," Sughrue said, "get going."

Valentine raised his head when the shooting stopped. He couldn't see where anyone was, and he was sure that he was now alone.

Ten-thousand dollars, he thought.

He rolled over onto his back, ejected the empty shells from his gun and reloaded.

Though people had poured out of the Long Branch to see what the commotion was, Dan Clark remained at his table.

After the first shot he had thought the job was done.

After the second shot, he was sure of it.

When it started to sound like an all out cavalry attack, he knew that Valentine had failed.

He got up and went into his office.

In the darkness Targett took his hand away from his wound and tightened his hand on his gun. He tried to ignore the pain in his shoulder, but it wasn't possible. He'd been shot before and he knew his wound would not be fatal with proper treatment.

When he got that treatment depended on how long Valentine eluded them.

Thirty-Four

"Valentine!"

"Are you still breathing, Targett?"

"I'm breathing."

"How bad did I get you?"

"Bad enough. I could bleed to death."

"Depends on when you get treatment, doesn't it?"

"That's right."

"And that depends on when you get me."

"Right again."

"Valentine, can you hear me?" came Tilghman's voice. The lawman had managed to get to his feet and was leaning against the side of the house. He couldn't see Valentine, but he could hear him He could also see Targett, and he knew he was wounded. He took a second to wonder about the welfare of Nixon and Sughrue after all the shooting that had occurred.

"I hear you, Tilghman."

"You haven't killed anybody yet, Valentine. You can still walk away from this."

"How can I do that?"

"Give me the man you're working for."

"If I tell you his name I can walk away?"

"Right out of town, but it's got to be now, Valentine. Right now!"

Valentine thought about it.

What did he owe Clark? The man was very likely planning to have *him* killed rather than pay him off.

And he liked the idea of walking away free—with the money Clark had paid him up front.

"Okay, Marshal, you've got a deal."

"What's the name?"

"Clark. Dan Clark."

"Ride, Valentine, and don't ever come back here."

"Don't worry, Marshal, I won't. You've got some crazy laws here."

Targett didn't like letting Valentine go free, but he knew why Tilghman did it, and it wasn't to get Clark's name. Tilghman already knew who Valentine worked for.

Tilghman wanted to get Targett off the street before he bled to death.

He watched as Valentine walked to the livery to saddle a horse and ride out of town. Sughrue actually passed close enough to touch the man—if he'd had a mind to—on his way to Targett's side. In a few moments Nixon joined them. Finally, Tilghman came limping up to them. They made a motley looking crew, to say the least, Nixon the only one who had escaped unscathed. Only one of Valentine's men had been killed, and the other two ran off.

"Are you all right?" Nixon asked, helping Targett to his feet.

"I'll be fine." He looked at Tilghman. "What happened to you?"

"I fell off the damn roof!" Tilghman said, daring anyone to comment on it.

"You didn't have to let him go on my account," Targett said.

"Your account?" Tilghman said. "Now what makes you think that?" He looked at Sughrue and said, "The sheriff needs medical attention, as well."

"I'm fine," Sughrue said. "Targett's hurt worse than me. The bleeding's already stopped."

Tilghman looked at Nixon and said, "Get them to the doctor."

"Right," Nixon said.

"You up to coming with me to get Dan Clark?" he asked Sughrue.

"That's my job," Sughrue said.

As Tilghman and Sughrue walked—or limped—away Targett said, "Let's not go to the doctor just yet, Tom . . ."

When Tilghman and Sughrue got to the Long Branch there were still some men out on the street waiting to find out what was going on.

"What happened, Marshal?" somebody asked.

"Anybody get killed, Sheriff?"

"Pat," Tilghman said, "why don't you see if you can't get everybody to go home."

"Sure, Bill."

As Tilghman walked back toward Clark's office he heard Sughrue telling Fred the bartender, "Closing time, Fred. Let's get everybody out."

Tilghman opened the door without knocking and walked in. Clark was seated behind his desk holding a snifter of brandy.

"Ah, Marshal," he said, "I've been expecting you."

"Let's go, Clark."

"Go where?"

"You're under arrest."

"For what?"

"Conspiracy to commit murder."

"That's rid—"

"The man you hired confessed in front of four witnesses," Tilghman said, "four peace officers. You can't get out of this one, Clark. Let's go."

"Can I finish this first?" Clark asked. "It's excellent brandy."

Tilghman walked to the desk and slapped the snifter out of

Clark's hand. The brandy went flying and the snifter smashed as it struck the floor.

"What the—"

"You're going to be doing without for a long time, Clark," Tilghman said, "You might as well start now."

Epilogue

Valentine had his horse saddled before he realized that the animal would not fit through the unlocked door. He was going to have to find the deputy, Nixon, and get him to open the front doors.

As he stepped out the back door somebody put a gun in his ear.

"Targett?"

"Yup."

"What are you doing?" he demanded. "I had a deal with the Marshal."

"That's right," Targett said, "you had a deal with the Marshal, not me."

"Hey," Valentine said. "you're not gonna take it personal that I shot you, are you. I was just doing my job, you know."

"I know," Targett said, "a job you were probably going to get paid very well for."

"Yeah, well, I can forget that now, huh? Listen, where's the deputy? He's got to open the front doors for me."

"There's one little thing before you leave, Valentine," Targett said.

"What's that?"

"The money Clark paid you."

"I told you—"

Don't kid me, Valentine," Targett said, pushing his gun further into the man's ear. "You wouldn't take a job on me without getting some of the money up front."

"I didn't get anything up front, Targett. Oh, I asked but Clark wouldn't come across—"

"Valentine, if I search you and come up with more than ten dollars I'm going to decide to take it *real* personal that you shot me."

There was a long moment of silence, then Valentine shrugged and said, "Well, easy come, easy go, right?"

He handed Targett the five-thousand dollars.

"This was half, huh?"

"Half."

"I'm flattered." Targett lifted his head and called out, "Okay, Tom, open the doors for the man." He took the gun away from Valentine's ear and said, "Have a nice ride, and you'd better hope our paths don't cross again."

"You got to stop taking things so personal, Targett," Valentine said.

Targett waited while Nixon opened the door, let Valentine out, and then locked them again. Nixon came over and caught him just before he fell down.

"Okay," Targett said, "now you can get me to a doctor."